MIAMI

by

HENRY MORGAN

CHIMERA

Miami Bound first published in 2002 by
Chimera Publishing Ltd
PO Box 152
Waterlooville
Hants
PO8 9FS

Printed and bound in Great Britain by
Omnia Books Ltd, Glasgow.

MIAMI BOUND

Henry Morgan

This novel is fiction – in real life practice safe sex

David picked up the pace, pushing firmly into her, relishing the feel of his prick cushioned by her wet feminine luxury.

'Big bad Ralph is a naughty man,' she added breathlessly. 'He ties me up and pushes things into me – all sorts of things. I'm a bad girl… you should spank me.'

Without any further tempting required, he smacked her bottom so hard it sent searing bolts of sensation surging through her delicate frame. She cried out as if unable to believe how much it hurt, and he spanked her again, and again, remembering how it felt to have his palm stinging as it made contact with hot flesh.

Chapter One

There is an American man in Wales, Alaska, who is a doppelganger for Grizzly Adams and, at the moment, he was beside David Harper pulling on the chewed remnants of a fat cigar. 'They're good,' he said from under his tan leather hat, 'and I've never seen such whopper tits on no Eskimo.'

'They're Lapps,' David corrected him for the third time in as many minutes.

'Lapps, Wops, Eskimos, they're all the same to me,' the big man retorted, 'but I sure to God ain't seen bigger tits than that on no Eskimo.'

Sighing, David gave up as Grizzly called for a bottle of bourbon.

A tall young woman with blonde hair down to her hips and very large breasts set a bottle of Wild Turkey down on the bar in front of them, and smiled as she filled their shot glasses. Grizzly didn't pay her, he didn't have to; it was his bar. Lock, stock and every barrel of beer, he owned it all. And if David felt comfortable enough leaving the two Lapps, Teena and Mishka, here with him, he would own them, too.

Bill – Grizzly's real name when he wasn't chopping trees and busting the heads of local drunks – poured them both a second shot. Then he shoved his stubby cigar back in his mouth, picked up the bottle of bourbon and motioned for David to follow him to a table.

'Tell me that bullshit story of yours again,' he demanded

in his usual blunt fashion once they were seated.

David sipped his drink, and grimaced. Bill knew he didn't like bourbon, yet he always ordered it for him. It was some sort of perverse ritual they had fallen into.

'What's up, bourbon too strong for you?' Grizzly taunted him. 'I'll get you a root beer if you want, but if it's that brown-and-black limey shit you're after, you're out of luck. I sold it all to the Eskimos. They use it to seal their canoes with.'

For all his rough talk, David knew Bill was an all right guy. But in this part of the world, it was wise to let people think you were always ready to scrape your knuckles off their chin if they fooled with you. 'I'd rather have a vodka,' he said.

Bill motioned with his hand, mouthed an order to the ever-attentive Trixie from Tuscola, and a bottle of *Absolute* arrived at their table a moment later. 'Why do you drink that shit-awful Russky stuff?' He pulled a disgusted face as he watched his English friend pour himself a shot of the clear liquor. 'You know they make it out of potato skins, don't you?'

'That's poteen,' David corrected him mildly, 'and the Irish make it.'

'It's the same fucking thing, a peasant's drink. Look at *this*.' He held up his glass of bourbon and allowed the dim light in the bar to shine through the lovely amber liquid. 'Says a bit more to you than that piss water, don't it?'

David swallowed his first shot of vodka, and sighed again, this time with pleasure. He waited a moment for the heat in his throat, and for the memories, to subside, and then poured out another shot straightaway.

Bill whistled a warning. 'Hey there, I said it was shit, I didn't say it wouldn't blow your balls off.'

David smiled, downed his shot as the big Alaskan eyed the two young women they were meeting about, and promptly poured a third.

Bill shook his head. 'Gets rid of the dreams, huh?'

'No more dreams,' David replied firmly. 'I left them all behind.'

'When you left that bitch behind… what's her name?'

'Sabrina.'

'Yeah. No wonder you like knocking back the drink. Why was she after you?'

Once again, David told Bill the story of the sex school he had run in England that taught women how to be good wives to their husbands, and of the young Pakistani girl, Sabrina, who was brought to him for training. His friend, Justin, had fallen in love with Sabrina, and the two of them had turned the tables and enslaved him.

'So, how come you ended up in Russia?'

'Because, they were taking me there anyway.'

This was the part of the story Bill liked best. 'Yeah,' he growled, half excited, half incredulous, 'they were taking you there to fuck women!'

'That's not the point. They treated me like I was a possession, like I was some sort of stud animal.'

'Yeah, but they were taking you there to fuck women.' Bill clearly didn't understand the problem. He picked up the bottle of vodka and refilled David's shot glass. 'She must have been one hell of a woman, this Sabrina.'

'She was a bitch.'

'Yeah, she was a bitch, but she was obviously one a hell of a woman, too. She must have been a knockout in the sack.'

David smiled, and gave up on the rest of the story. 'In the sack, over the chair and dangling from the ceiling, but she paid me back, *big* time. She tried to sell me. She chased me across Russia after I escaped, and almost killed me on that frozen fucking sea. She was a hell of a woman, all right, and she almost dragged us all there with her.'

Bill looked around his club. A group of oil workers in Stetson hats were gathered around the stage along with half-a-dozen Arapahos. They all worked in the oil fields, and they all had money in their pockets they were quickly transferring to the hips of Teena and Mishka as rock music belted out of the jukebox. *I'm gonna run to you*, he sang as the girls gyrated from one overpaid oil monkey to another, letting each man shove greenbacks into their panties, and cop a feel of their tight young bottom as they ground it in the face of their whiskey-fuelled fantasy.

'How come you went back and rescued that other guy from the ice?' Bill asked abruptly. 'That's what I can't figure out.'

'Because he was a good mate,' David said, 'and if you'd seen Sabrina, you'd have done the same.'

'But how do you know he ain't gonna double-cross you again now he's back in England?'

'Why should he?'

'Because he's done it before?'

'He simply mislaid his loyalties in Russia,' David defended his old friend, Justin. 'A lot of people did. No, he'll sell the house in Cornwall and fly out to meet me in Miami, as we agreed.'

'With the money?'

'With the money.'

'So, what are you going to do between now and then, besides make even more money when we've closed on these Wops of yours?'

Laughing, David shook his head and raised his glass in

the direction of the two dancing girls.

The sisters spotted his gesture, and waved back at him happily.

'You know what I'm going to do, Bill? I'm going to get me some sun on my back and spend some of my money. I'm gonna get myself the biggest RV I can find and I'm going to see the good old US of A. I'm gonna drink some beer and screw some ass. How's that?' he demanded in his best imitation of a thick Yankee drawl.

Grizzly raised his glass in a salute. 'Sounds fine to me, I just wish I was coming with you.'

'Well, you can't. And you know why you can't? Because you've got a bar to run, bills to pay and a shit-load of money to make.'

'Is that good or bad?'

'I think it's both. When the money's tight and the repo-man knows your first name, you're going to think about me on a beach somewhere and say to yourself, "that should be me". But if it's you out there talking to the birds as you piss in the bushes, you're going to remember these nights in the bar with everyone buzzing and shouting "hi, Bill", "hey, Bill", "what you doing, Bill?" and then you're going to wish you were right here where you are now.'

Grizzly shook his head. 'You spent too much time in that goddamned snow, buddy.'

Their conversation was interrupted by several oil workers surging to their feet and calling for the bull.

Bill grinned. 'The boys want some fun with the girls. If they do all right, then it's a deal, ten grand.'

'You said twenty,' David reminded him.

'I thought you didn't care about money.'

David slapped him on the shoulder. 'I'm learning, my friend. You can't be in this country for long and not learn the importance of King Green.'

'Tell you what, we'll call it fifteen and I'll wipe your bar slate clean.'

'That's *no* deal,' David moaned.

Bill took the bottle of vodka from his friend, and held it up for him to look at. 'You seen your bar tab lately, buddy?'

From her position behind the bar, Trixie saw a few of the oil workers pulling out the bull and motioned to the manager with her hand. He responded with a broad smile, promptly loaded a Blue Oyster Cult tape into the deck, and hit *play*. Then he helped drag out the safety mats while the girls shimmied their way around the crowd collecting yet more bills, which they hurriedly folded into a secret pocket in their hats as they prepared for the ride. The trim young Lapps stood in front of the bull wearing nothing but G-string panties, rhinestone boots and brave smiles as they raised their hats up high.

'Now listen hear, you cowpokes and sons of whiskey-swilling bitches,' the bar manager shouted, 'I've got two girls here who don't fear the Reaper, little Miss Teena and little Miss Mishka!' He stepped up between them and pulled hard on their G-strings, which came off in his hands to reveal two perfectly clean-shaven pussies.

There was a great roar, and a dozen or more hats flew up towards the beams of the maple-vaulted ceiling as the men surrounded the bull, and the girls set off on a run around the inside of the circle of bodies, slapping away the hands reaching for them. Each girl must have received twenty to thirty slaps across her bare bottom before Mishka finally turned in, and vaulted onto the bull in one grand leap.

The men went wild, and their cheering escalated to a deafening volume when Teena launched herself at the bull's head. She gripped its horns, and swung her legs around its neck facing it.

All eyes were fixed on the girls' breasts as the bull began to move, its speed gradually increasing before it abruptly came to a stop, and reversed direction. A moment later, breasts and arms followed this change of course, and as the speed increased again so did the crowd's expectation.

Teena's grip on the bull grew tighter, her hat fell off, and all the while it looked as if the animal's angry snout was rooting hungrily into her pussy. The men roared with excitement as the girls struggled to stay on, and although their audience had no way of knowing it, they had both drifted back into memories of their childhood riding caribou in the tribe's games. They hung on for dear life, oblivious to the ribald shouts and leering stares of the men around them. The manager cruelly wound up the power, and Grizzly Bill stepped forward to admire the girls' abilities. David was not so surprised by it; he knew them well. In fact, he was intimately acquainted with both of them.

At maximum power, both girls stayed on the bull longer than anyone else ever had. Mishka was the first to be thrown off onto the mat, and a moment later Teena was launched like a huge starfish into the crowd. They were immediately pulled to their feet, handed back their hats, and lifted onto broad shoulders they rode triumphantly without effort. One lucky oil worker got to feel the heat of Teena's hot young sex lips pressed against the back of his neck as he carried her over to the bar, where both girls were cheerfully hosed down with beer.

'Goddamn it!' Bill exclaimed. 'Did you see those Wops? Did you see them?!'

'I told you they were good.' David smiled as he headed back towards their table.

'Did you see the way they gripped that bull? Jesus, they

11

could crack coconuts with them thighs. I could clean up in this shit-hole with them two girls.'

'Worth every bit of that twenty grand,' David agreed.

Bill sat down across from him again, poured out two shots of vodka, and smiled. 'Worth every nickel, except we already settled on fifteen.' He knocked back his drink, realised it was vodka, and cursed long and loud. 'That's all you deserve for drinking this piss! You got no standards. What would you do with another five grand, anyway?'

The manager announced that the show was over to disappointed groans, but they were short-lived as a tall blonde girl trotted out onto the stage, and began gyrating to another track blasting from the tape deck. Like moths attracted to the light of a lovely fire, the men drifted back towards the stage and watched, half hypnotized, as she slowly began stripping for them.

'Is it a deal then?' Bill asked.

David had already made up his mind. He was leaving in the morning. He had let the girls dance tonight in order to watch their reaction. If they hadn't enjoyed themselves, he would have taken them with him, but he could see they relished the freedom of the American lifestyle. When he first met them, they were living a quiet existence in northern Russia following a herd of deer, their lives governed by the seasons – long cold winters and a few short and glorious months of summer. The winters were just as cold here in Alaska but lit up by the bright neon signs of countless bars and casinos. The roads were paved and people drove expensive sports utility vehicles. All these things excited the girls, as did their new western clothing, and the discovery that men would pay handsomely to watch them take it all off.

'It's a deal,' David announced, just as the girls turned up

at the table and sat down on either side of them. They had washed the beer off and changed into short denim skirts and cotton shirts, over which they were still wearing their beloved cowboy hats.

'Great,' Bill declared. 'Let's celebrate.'

'What are we celebrating?' Teena asked.

Bill rolled his eyes up into his skull in mock rapture. 'God, I *love* that accent.'

That was something else the girls had learned quickly; their English was now nearly perfect, and tinged with a sexy foreign lilt men seemed to find irresistible.

'Bill says it's okay for you to stay with him,' David told her.

'But what about you?' Mishka asked solemnly.

David hesitated. He knew the sisters felt very close to him and would be saddened by his departure, but there was no easy way to break the news. 'I'm leaving in the morning,' he said bluntly, 'and heading south.'

As he had expected, both girls suddenly looked glum.

'Hey,' Bill said brightly, 'I'll take care of you.'

They looked to David for confirmation.

'You'll be safe with Bill,' he assured them. 'He's your new man now. You must do as he says just as you always did for me. Whatever he asks you to do, you'll do, and you'll never question him, just like I taught you.'

The sisters nodded, but continued to sulk.

'Come on girls, this is happy town,' Grizzly said. 'You and me, we'll make a fortune. You'll have everything you want.'

This promise cheered the sisters up somewhat, and Teena asked tentatively, 'Anything?'

'Anything,' her new owner answered firmly, 'as long as you're good girls.'

13

'That's settled then,' David said. 'They're always good girls.'

The mood of the table lifted, and Bill suggested they head back to his lodge to cement the deal.

Grizzly's home sat back from the road on the outskirts of town only a few minutes' drive from the bar. There were no lights on inside except for those of his security system, which kicked in the moment they turned onto the drive.

Teena promptly leapt out from the back seat, and ran her hand admiringly along the paintwork of the four-by-four. 'Can I have one of these?' she asked sweetly.

Bill put his arm around her. 'Baby, you keep jiggling those nice big tits of yours the way you did tonight, and you can have a whole fucking fleet of them.'

On the walk down his driveway, Teena showed him just how good she could jiggle her breasts, and Bill laughed cheerfully.

From the outside, the lodge looked like a large trapper's cabin, but on the inside it was comfortably modern. A huge stone fireplace took up one entire wall of the living room, and from above the mantel a mounted moose's head stared balefully down into the room. Bill turned a key, and a moment later the room was bathed in the warm glow of firelight. It was a comfortable space that immediately made the girls feel at home. Two large overstuffed sofas covered with Indian throws faced each other in front of the hearth, and between them lay the outstretched pelt of a snarling polar bear. Mishka giggled when she saw it, and said something to her sister in their native tongue. Both girls then sank to their hands and knees on the bear's back and buried their faces in its soft white fur.

The two men stepped closer to the fire to better admire

the tight young bottoms on display, for the girls' skirts hiked up around their hips as they bent forward.

'I'm going to miss this view,' David said thoughtfully.

'I'll write you about it,' Bill teased him, and went for some drinks. When he returned, the two girls were sitting on the sofa across from David, who was talking to them about what he expected them to do now that they were his friend's property. The two sisters were listening intently, and nodding every now and then to show him that they understood.

'Everything okay?' Bill queried, handing David his drink and sitting down next to him.

'Fine. I was just explaining their duties to them.'

'That's good. I'd rather get off on the right foot than have to teach them from scratch. I'm getting a bit too long in the tooth for all that.' He nodded towards a large leather belt draped across the back of a chair. 'But it is there if I need it.'

'I'm sure you won't.' David sipped his drink. 'Unless you want to spice things up a bit,' he added, and told the girls it was time to show the goods.

The sisters pulled their feet up onto the sofa, bent their knees and sat with their legs slightly parted. Both their pussies were freshly shaved.

'Had them sheared this morning,' David said. 'Hope you like it.'

'Would have done it myself,' Bill replied. 'Only hair between them legs is going to be my beard. I think I'd like to see some more of them sweet tits now and grab me some nice young ass. After all, I sure as hell paid enough for it.' He rose and set his glass of bourbon down on the mantle while the girls unbuttoned their shirts, and then he sat down between them on the sofa.

15

Teena and Mishka each had full round breasts that looked like mirror images of each other's. Grizzly revelled in their soft firmness, marvelling at the way they pushed back into his hand when he squeezed them. 'Gonna miss this?' he asked cruelly.

David got up, and began taking off his clothes. 'For old time's sake,' he said, and tugged Mishka to her feet. Bill had pulled out his prick, and now he sat Teena down on it facing her away from him. The girl bounced happily up and down on his rigid pole as he spread her thighs wider, offering an excellent view of his thrusting cock to the other couple.

'Down you go,' David commanded, and pushed Mishka down onto her knees. There was only one place for her head to go, and that was between her sister's legs.

Teena smiled happily. She had her pussy filled, and now she could see a tongue licking its way towards her clit. Grizzly's big cock had forced her young hole into a tight oval around it, and her slippery lips hugged its veined length tightly. Then Mishka's tongue explored his ball sac and his penis swelled even more in response to the delicious sensation. He moaned deep in his throat, and feeling the extra girth, Teena moaned, too. Then Mishka and David echoed their earthy mumblings as he knelt behind her and pushed his weapon into her silky sheath.

David was accustomed to using the girls for his own pleasure, but tonight was the last time he would see them naked, the last time he would smell their musk, the last time he would fuck their sweet young cunts. He settled his cock inside Mishka and let it soak up the moist warmth of her innermost flesh. He waited for her response, and it came in the form of the tiniest push against his hips. He slid out along her passage, and then slipped back in even more deeply, until the tip of his glands nudged the limits of her hot, dark space. The contact flowed from cock to cunt, and from cunt to tongue, and then from tongue to cock, and when Bill's erection pulsed and passed its message to Teena, the circle was complete.

For a long time they carried on with the cycle of taking pleasure and passing it on at a relaxed pace. There was to be no pounding tonight, no leather, no whipping. It was gentle sex, and the girls received it gratefully.

David had forced them to serve many a cruel man, and he had been free and easy with the leather in the early weeks of his ownership of them. No doubt Bill would resort to the belt from time to time himself. The sisters were new to America and to the West, and they would get out of line as all women did from time to time, but their new owner would dole out his punishments wisely. These girls would make him rich, and in return he would allow them to enjoy all the benefits of capitalism. Teena would get her four-by-four, and Mishka her own cabin on the shore looking out towards the motherland.

But that was all in the future, and tonight David had a lot of memories to go through.

The rental car arrived earlier than David would have liked. Bill drew back the curtains, and signalled the driver that he had heard his irritatingly loud horn. The naked girls remained peacefully asleep on his king-size bed. He observed David's sad expression as he dressed, and said, 'I'll leave you alone with them.'

'No, I don't think I'll wake them,' David quietly refused the offer. 'I said enough last night. They'll understand, wont they?'

'They're big girls,' Bill pointed out, 'and you can't look

after them forever.' He left the room to invite the young man from the rental car agency in for waffles and coffee while he waited.

David, however, refused the offer of breakfast when he appeared in the kitchen a short while later, ready to go.

'That's it then,' Bill said gruffly.

'Guess so.'

They shook hands warmly, and David headed for the door.

'Forgetting something?' Bill called after him. 'Like your money, for instance?'

David laughed, and wondered for a moment if he had forgotten on purpose, so he would not feel guilty about selling two girls he had grown so fond of.

Bill pulled a holdall out from beneath the sink. 'Don't feel guilty,' he said, his advice betraying a sensitive insight into people's thoughts no one would suspect of him.

'Look after them for me,' David said.

'No worries.' Bill handed him his cash. 'Keep in touch.'

Chapter Two

There were many ways to get to Miami, but David was not acquainted with any of them. Obviously he could fly there, but where was the fun in that? From point A to point B and a nice selection of clouds to admire on the way. He wasn't due to meet up with Justin for some time, therefore he decided he would make the trip the old-fashioned way, the pioneer's way... well, almost. He would get himself an RV and drive to Miami. But during his travels, he had learned the hard way about distances, so he did in fact make the first leg of his journey by plane.

He flew to Seattle from Spenard airfield in the early hours of a May morning. The sky was jet-black and the stars looked close enough to reach. The wheels touched down on cool tarmac, and the gentle bump woke a dozing salesman who was clutching his bag like a comforter. He saw David watching him, and the two exchanged polite greetings before the plane's engines roared their protest at being forced to a stop.

Outside the airport, David jumped into one of the waiting cabs and asked to be taken to a restaurant on the water. The driver loved these kinds of fares, and spoke eagerly into his radio trying to find out who was giving a kickback for delivering a customer. He got his few extra bucks, the *Lobster Pot* got their customer, and David got great views of the ocean.

The nip in the air sent him inside the building to a table by the window, where he ordered a beer and a lobster, which was delivered to him lying peacefully on a bed of lettuce. He thanked the waitress, and made good with the pliers.

Seattle was not that far south, but he suddenly found himself regaining his sense of smell. The frozen north seemed to deny aromas their existence as nothing decayed up there; flesh remained flesh until something came along to consume it. Here, however, the oil of the harbour and the scent of the sea demanded his attention. It gave him a rush of sensation as he snapped a claw open and sucked out the meat. He had his teeth in the muscle when he noticed a waiflike young woman watching him from outside. She was balanced on the harbour wall, and she looked very hungry.

David was not a stranger to loneliness. Before he met Teena and Mishka, his had been a solitary existence. He saw at once that this girl knew what it was like to be alone; her expression spoke of a hunger for companionship as much as for food, so he took up the long two-pronged fork, pulled the last of the meat out of the claw, and gestured to her to come and eat.

The girl looked nervously at him for a moment before obeying his summons, but then she hesitated again at the entrance to the restaurant. Her clothes were unwashed and her hair was unkempt, but David saw past all that. Clothes made the man, beauty sold the woman. He motioned to her again, and she shook her head. He persisted and, finally, she took the momentous step inside. When the hostess intercepted her she pointed towards David, who smiled his approval. He had eaten at the best tables and scavenged scraps from the floor, and he knew people were more important than menus. He held the hostess's eyes and, after hesitating for a long moment, she allowed the girl to pass.

'Hungry?' he asked when she finally arrived at his table.

She lied by shaking her head, and then sat across from him, silently watching him eat, for nearly ten minutes. He did not force conversation. If nothing else, at least she was in out of the cold. It was his waitress who pressed the moment.

'Will the young lady be eating?' she asked pointedly.

'I don't know,' he replied. 'Are you dining tonight, darling?'

The girl smiled at him, and shook her head again.

'You must take some nourishment, my dear,' David said in his most refined English accent. 'Surely those bullies at the magazine can't expect you to starve. Forget the pictures. Let them get someone else, I say. See if Claudia will do it. Or Naomi. You work much too hard on your image for those beastly photographers. Do try the shrimp avocado.'

The silent waif surprised him by replying, in plum English tones, that the shrimp avocado would be just fine. And a few minutes later, when the dish was set before her, she valiantly resisted the temptation to shove the whole lot into her mouth.

David leaned across the table and whispered, 'Well done.'

She giggled, and accepted his offer of wine.

'Warmer now?' he enquired.

'Much,' she replied, and kept on eating.

He ordered dessert, a fruit boat for himself and a death-by-chocolate cake for her. After years in the tundra, he craved fruit. The cake he ordered simply because it was packed with calories, and the girl needed them.

'Where do you go from here?' he asked her as she wolfed down her dessert. He could risk talking now; if she bolted, at least she would do so on a full stomach.

'I'll find a boat,' she replied quietly.

There was something unusual about her that attracted

21

David. She had long dark hair parted in the middle and big brown eyes. She kept tucking one side of her hair behind one ear, but left the rest hanging over her right eye in a way that made him think of a puppy peering shyly out from behind a curtain. She did not seem the sort of girl who was accustomed to spending time on the streets.

'No home?' he pursued his gentle enquiry.

'A long ways back,' she said, staring dramatically into space. 'A long, long ways.'

He smiled ruefully. 'Not too long, I imagine.'

She cocked her head to one side, intensifying the puppy dog look, clearly wondering how he knew.

'Your jeans,' David explained. 'You're living rough, but they still don't have any holes in them. I don't see a bag, so I assume you have all your worldly possessions about your person. And you don't have a coat because you don't have anywhere to leave your things. All you own is what you're wearing, which leads me to assume you left home about two weeks ago, just enough time to develop the charming street urchin look, but not enough time to think like one.'

'*Three* weeks,' she corrected him, trying not to look impressed by his powers of deduction.

'Husband?'

She shook her head, and quickly scraped up the remains of the sinful cake.

'Boyfriend?'

She was a lot more relaxed now with alcohol, sugar and chocolate socialising in her veins. 'Wrong again.'

'Then I've pried enough.'

'That's all right, I owe you an explanation for the meal.'

Their waitress appeared again. 'Can I get you two anything else?'

They had outstayed their welcome. David glanced at his

watch. It was one-thirty in the morning. He paid the bill, and retrieved his rucksack from the cloakroom.

The girl laughed when she saw it. 'Does that make two of us on the streets?'

'If I can't find somewhere to stay,' he replied serenely.

They stepped outside, and began walking away from the restaurant. They had only gone about ten feet when the lights went out behind them, leaving them spotlighted beneath a street lamp.

'So,' she shivered and hugged herself, 'thanks for the meal.'

'My pleasure.'

The inevitable awkwardness followed.

'I'll be off now,' she said, and stepped off the sidewalk onto the road.

'Where will you stay?'

'I told you, a boat. There's always someone who forgets to lock their cabin.'

'There's no need for that. I'm booking a room in a hotel. Why don't you stay with me?'

Her eyes betrayed how tempted she was by the offer even as she asked suspiciously, 'How do I know you're not crazy?'

'Because you're still not a real homeless girl and you have wits enough left not to fall into such a stupid trap.'

'Stupid traps are usually the most lethal,' she replied with remarkable astuteness for her age, but she stepped back onto the sidewalk beside him. 'Where's the hotel?'

'Ah, you see, this is where you earn your room and board. I haven't got a clue. You'll have to suggest one.'

'I know the perfect place,' she declared at once. 'It looks out over Elliot Bay. You'll love it. But we'll have to take a cab.'

'There can't be that many hotels still using oil lamps,' David remarked appreciatively.

'I know, that's why it's so special. I told you, didn't I?'

David took in the antique wrought iron bed framing a large and lumpy down-filled mattress, and a long chaise lounge against one wall, as his guide opened a pair of French doors leading out onto a first floor balcony overlooking the harbour. The full moon, hanging low in the sky this late at night, cast a glimmering silver path of light across the black water.

'That's wonderful, too,' she whispered, stepping outside.

David grabbed two cushions off the lounge, and joined her. He threw them down onto the concrete floor and kicked them close together.

'I wonder what's out there,' she said dreamily, sinking down onto one of the cushions and gazing out over the water.

David opened his rucksack, and pulled out a metal flask along with the bone cup that remained one of his few treasured possessions. Then he sat down beside her, filled the cup with vodka, and offered it to her. She took a quick sip, and handed it back to him.

They repeated this ritual several times before he got up and stepped back into the room. He returned with a blanket he used to cover them both as he sank down beside her again, and leaned comfortably back against the wall.

'You've been to lots of places,' she said. 'I can tell.'

'A few,' he admitted. 'What about you?'

'Me?' She laughed. 'I've never been south of Eugene.'

'Is that why you ran away?'

'Sort of… that, and other things…'

'You don't have to tell me.'

'That's all right… my mom's boyfriend kept hitting on

me. Whenever she left the room he'd start saying things.'

'That must have been bad,' he commiserated.

'I could handle it, but then she said they were getting married and that he'd be my new dad. After that he stopped talking and started touching me whenever he got the chance, brushing up against me when I passed him in the hall, and things like that. I told him to stop it, but he said he was family now.'

'Why didn't you tell your mother about it?'

'She wouldn't have believed me. She was in love with him. And whenever she was around he'd be real careful not to let on what he was doing. So, I thought, what the heck, I'm nineteen now, and I left.'

'And how do you reckon you're doing?'

'God awful!' She laughed again, and took another sip of vodka. Then she returned the cup to him and leaned her body against his.

'Have you let your mother know you're safe?'

Her firm, 'No,' was echoed by the deep bellow of a foghorn somewhere out in the bay.

'She'll be worried,' David said matter-of-factly. 'You should tell her you're safe.'

'I can't trust myself to. She'll ask me why I ran away, and I'll end up telling her that Ted was putting his hand up my skirt, and we'll start arguing.' She looked up at a plane passing overhead. 'More people going some place. I wish it was me.'

'No you don't,' David said flatly. 'You wish you were home with your mother eating pancakes and watching television. Besides, runaways don't go north, they head south to sunny California. They don't hang around the Seattle harbour freezing their arses off.' He poured some more vodka into the cup. 'That's *ass* to you, I believe.'

There was a loud clatter a few feet away from the balcony, and they both leapt to their feet in time to see a drunk picking himself up from between two trashcans he had stumbled into.

'Your future,' he said. 'Unless you're careful.'

'I'll get by.' She sat down again. 'Sooner or later, something will come up. I'll get a job. I might do some modelling, like you were saying in the restaurant. You must think I could do it or you wouldn't have made that joke.'

'Well then, maybe the street's the best place for you right now.' He resumed his place beside her on the cushions. 'If you can learn to look after yourself there, you should be able to handle all the men who'll promise you anything in return for a few favours.'

'I know all about them already, that's why I sleep on boats.'

'Oh?' The tone in her voice suggested to him that she was not quite as naïve as he had believed her to be. 'What do you mean?'

'I learned fast.' She took a long swig of vodka. 'My first night in the harbour, I slept on a boat because I thought I'd be safe. I thought people who owned boats were rich and decent and wouldn't kick me off. I was so tired that when I found an unlocked cabin, I just sneaked in and went straight to sleep. I didn't even use one of the beds because I didn't want to make a mess.'

'And what happened then?'

'The owner came back. I broke down and told him everything, and he said I could stay on the boat if I kept it tidy and did a few things for him.'

'What sort of things?' David asked sharply, and when she didn't answer, he began questioning his earlier appraisal of her. He was spot-on about so much, yet he obviously had a lot more to learn. 'How did you reply to his offer?'

'I let him do what he wanted,' she answered quietly. 'I was desperate.'

David shifted his position and sat facing her, his back to Elliot Bay. 'So, he let you sleep on his boat if you had sex with him?'

'It was like a business deal,' she said defensively. 'He'd come around in the morning and fuck me before he went to work.'

His jaw dropped at the casual way she said the word 'fuck'. This lovely young woman, who obviously knew so little about anything, admitted to being fucked as if she were merely talking about mowing the lawn.

'But then he got sort of kinky,' she went on, 'and said I had to put it in my mouth. I didn't really want to, but I could tell he loved it. He was a lot older than me, in his late forties, maybe even his early fifties.'

'Was it his boat you were going back to tonight?'

'No, I left that behind me. Now I just sleep on the boats in secret. I left him after he brought his work buddies over one night.'

'Did he share you with them?'

'Yeah, he did,' she answered coolly, 'but I did it just that once; pulled a train for them, I mean.'

David was having trouble controlling his swelling penis. His intentions had been good from the beginning, but the way she was talking was inevitably affecting him. The problem was he could not be sure she knew what she was doing; her casual attitude might only be a brave act. 'So…' he cleared his throat in a vain effort to alleviate some of his growing physical tension, 'you didn't stay on the boat?'

'No. Bob made it perfectly clear that while I was on his boat, I had to obey his rules. If his friends were coming over to catch a train, I had to be at the station. So the morning after the gangbang, I was *out* of there.' She pulled a pack of cigarettes from her shirt pocket, and offered him one.

He had given up smoking when he couldn't get any Loki in Wales, but he sensed now was the moment to start up again. He accepted the cigarette, and then the lighter she handed him. They exhaled their first drags simultaneously, their breaths mingling in the air between them as he remarked, 'Bit of a shock for a country girl. I'm surprised you never caught the next bus home.'

'I'm surprised myself,' she confessed. 'But once you've crossed that line, it all gets easier. I even sort of liked it when Bob and his friends were encouraging me by telling me how beautiful I was.' With her free hand she began undoing the buttons of her shirt. 'I was always embarrassed because I thought I had small breasts, but Bob loved them, and so did his friends. They kept saying they were perfect, like little apples in their hands.' She pulled open her shirt and revealed a white bra that almost seemed to glow in the moonlight. 'What do *you* think?'

'They look fine to me.'

She tugged her bra down and exposed both her breasts, which suited her petite frame perfectly. They were round and firm, and the dark stems of her nipples did indeed evoke snow-covered apples. She took a drag of her cigarette, and blew the smoke down over her bosom.

David's penis grew even thicker inside his trousers, demanding to be released and allowed to do its work. He fought to control his desire, but failed miserably when she shrugged off her shirt and pulled her bra off completely. Then she stood up and held the cigarette between her lips to unbuckle her jeans. She began pushing them down, and her white panties followed the tight denim so her curly dark pubic hair sneaked into view.

'Oops,' she giggled, tossing her cigarette carelessly over the balcony, 'I showed you too much.'

David was silent as she held her panties up with one hand and shoved her tight jeans down with the other. 'I just wanted to see if you liked my ass.' She turned around, placed her hands flat against the hotel wall, and pushed her bottom out towards him. The moonlight reflected off her white cotton underwear. 'Well?' she asked, a note of uncertainty creeping into her flirtatious tone as he remained silent.

Her buttocks were young and firm and curved out nicely in all the right places. 'Lovely,' he said, and drawing deeply on his cigarette slowly exhaled the word, 'Beautiful…'

'Of course, it might look even better if I was naked,' she suggested softly.

He swallowed hard; his throat was dry, and it was not from the cigarette smoke. 'It might,' he agreed quietly. 'I think you should let me see it.'

'Without my panties?'

'Yes.' He adjusted his trousers to accommodate the hard-on pressing against his zipper.

'Well… okay.' Still facing the wall, she slipped her panties all the way down to her ankles. Then she pulled off her sneakers and stepped out of both her jeans and her undergarment, kicking them both aside carelessly.

'Why don't you bend over,' he suggested as casually as he could.

She pushed herself away from the wall, spread her legs, and reached down for her ankles. 'Like this?' she asked coyly.

In the moonlight the rich folds of her pussy glistened

with a wet pink sheen, and a small dark space revealed the entrance to her body's innermost shrine. This girl had been stretched, and recently. David carefully put out his cigarette, inched himself forward, and inhaled her fragrance. She smelled strong and musky; she had obviously been fucked within the last day or two. He moved closer… the scent of sex mingled with perspiration and perfume was stronger now. His tongue reached out, and touched the tangy lips of her labia – the smooth, firm and deliciously soft satin curtains protecting the dark portal leading into the mysteries of her flesh. And above them beckoned the puckered starfish of her anus. He licked her again, tasting the slick and salty juices of her young pussy.

She moaned and pushed her vulva back into his face.

He grabbed hold of her hips, and penetrated her sphincter with the tip of his nose as his tongue lashed deep and hard into her cleft.

She let go of her ankles and braced herself against the wall, keeping her legs perfectly straight and her pussy directly in line with his penetrating tongue. She panted and whimpered as he ate her, and it wasn't long before her whole body tensed in the grip of an orgasm that seemed to wrench itself out of her flesh like a possessing spirit wailing across the Seattle skyline. She sank down onto her hands and knees, and David lost no time. He barely noticed freeing his rigid penis from its confinement as it swiftly found its way home to the centre of its universe – a warm pussy. He slipped his arms around her and fondled her breasts as he rode her lovely body. She parted for him easily, allowing him smooth passage as she moved in rhythm with him.

'You're a little loose,' he scolded her. 'Someone's been here before me.'

'Ralph,' she murmured contentedly. 'Big bad Ralph.'

30

David picked up the pace, pushing firmly into her, relishing the feel of his prick cushioned by her wet feminine luxury.

'Big bad Ralph is a naughty man,' she added breathlessly. 'He ties me up and pushes things into me – all sorts of things. I'm a bad girl… you should spank me.'

Without any further tempting required, he smacked her bottom so hard it sent searing bolts of sensation surging through her delicate frame. She cried out as if unable to believe how much it hurt, and he spanked her again, and again, remembering how it felt to have his palm stinging as it made contact with hot flesh.

'Oh, God,' she moaned, 'harder… please…'

Her prayer was answered with a vengeance as he grabbed a fistful of her hair, pulled her head back, and delivered an almighty smack across her taut young buttocks.

Waves of pain and pleasure crashed together in the centre of her body, and she screamed as an orgasm momentarily released her from the exquisite agony.

David kept riding her, picking up speed and energy without losing control. Fighting the desire to release his sperm he slowed his movements, and eventually slipped out of her hot pussy. The cool ocean breeze caressed his erection, which glistened with her juices and his own semen in the moonlight. She slumped forward the instant he pulled out of her, and he turned her over onto her back. Her perky little breasts defied gravity to point skywards, and he knelt there enjoying the sight of her for a moment. Then he found the pack of cigarettes in her shirt, sat back against the wall again, and lit one. He blew the smoke over her head, and she lazily raised her hand. He handed her the cigarette, and then lit another one for himself.

She took a drag, pulling her knees up until the soles of

her feet rested flat on the floor, giving David a glorious view of her fur-covered mound and the mysterious smile of thanks between her thighs.

'So, who's Big Bad Ralph?' he asked.

'Just someone I met after Bob. But he was different. He showed me stuff I'd never even dreamed of.'

'What sort of stuff, exactly?'

'Well, a few days after I left Bob, I found Ralph's boat, *Arctic Lady*. It was a big white cruiser with a sail and an engine. I slept on it for two nights before Ralph turned up and, just like with Bob, I told him everything.'

David's cock jumped in his hand as his mind filled with images. 'And what did he do to you?'

'He closed the door behind him, and started the engine. I asked him what he was doing, and he said he was taking me to the harbourmaster to call the police.'

'But he didn't.'

'No, he took me out to Puget Sound and anchored off Three Tree Point. When I asked him what he was doing again, he said he was collecting two nights' worth of rent. I told him it was all right, that I knew how to pay the rent, but he said he wanted something special. I got a little scared then, but I started getting undressed anyway. I just expected him to ride me for a bit and then let me go.' Her nipples were still erect from the lingering afterglow of sex and the caress of the cold night air. 'He told me to strip off my bra and panties while he watched, and he told me to do it slowly, because we had plenty of time.'

'How much time?'

'All weekend. He spent two whole days and nights fucking me all over his boat, and not just fucking me, either.'

David stroked his cock. 'How did it start?'

'With a blowjob, and while I was on my knees, he told

me I would be his personal property until I paid back what I owed him. I didn't like the way he was talking so I blew him really hard and tried to get him to come thinking it might calm him down, but the harder I sucked, the angrier he got. He said my cunt was his now, and that he could use it any way he wanted to.'

David closed his eyes. His mind transported him onboard the *Arctic Lady* as he slowly stroked his erection, keeping himself at the stage which years of denial had taught him how to reach – that mysterious plateau just before the inevitable moment of release. Then, suddenly, he felt her hand on his penis, and opened his eyes to discover her face was very close to his, and she was staring at him intently.

'He tied me to a bed in one of the cabins,' she went on quietly. 'I felt so helpless… he squeezed the back of my neck, pushed me facedown across the bed, and used belts to spread-eagle me.

'Then he went away, and it seemed like he was gone for ages.

'My mind was racing, but that's what he wanted. He wanted me to recognise how helpless I was. He wanted me to imagine all the things he could do to me.

'When he finally came back, he had a bottle of rum with him. He sat in a chair near my face and talked to me while he poured himself a drink. He said young runaways like me needed discipline. He said he was going to teach me how to be a good girl instead of a piece of street trash. I saw him undoing his belt and thought he was going to get on top of me, but he just lay the belt over my ass and sat down again.'

'He was taking his time,' David explained, enjoying the feel of her soft hand moving absently down his rigid penis as she told him her story. 'The guy sounds like he knew what he was doing.'

'He knew all right. He was jerking himself off real slow describing how he was going to strap my bottom for using his boat without his permission. I was trembling I was so scared, and he liked that; he said it showed I had respect. He promised I'd be okay as long as I paid him plenty of respect.'

'And that made you feel better?'

'Oh yes,' she answered fervently. 'I knew there was a way out now. But then he put his drink down and picked up the belt.'

'How many lashes did he give you?'

'Ten, maybe a dozen, I lost count. The stings all melted together until my ass felt like it was on fire.'

'But it felt good, too, didn't it?'

'I knew you'd understand,' she whispered, stroking his cock fervently. 'You seem to know so much about me, and we've only just met.'

'We've met before, darling, all over the world.'

She looked deep into his eyes, searching for an explanation.

'I'll show you,' he said, and stood up slowly as she continued nursing his cock in her hand. 'Come with me.'

She let go of him reluctantly and followed him back inside to the bed.

'Bend over,' he commanded.

She obeyed him, reaching for the posts on the footboard, and he began tying her wrists to it with belts he produced from his rucksack.

'You loved being helpless,' he told her. 'You loved not having a choice. You didn't have to feel guilty because none of it was your fault. No matter what he did to you, no one could say you had asked for it. All you could do was let him please himself, and that pleased you.'

She nodded and bit the bedcovers, bracing herself for the pain she knew was coming.

David pulled up a chair, sat directly behind her, and parted the cheeks of her firm young bottom with both hands to examine the enticing little starfish of her arsehole. It was not as tight as he would have expected it to be in a girl so young; it, too, had been stretched and used recently. He kept his voice cool and even as he asked, 'What did he do with the bottle after he beat you?'

'He poured rum over my ass.'

'Did it sting?'

'Like a thousand bees!' she exclaimed, and then the sudden slap of his hand made her yelp and bite the bedcovers again; Ralph had denied her the release of crying out and she remembered the lesson only too well.

'Did it feel good?' David spanked her again.

She emptied her mouth of cotton long enough to gasp, 'Yes!'

'And where was the bottle?'

She did not answer.

He smacked her a third time and patiently repeated the question, smiling to himself. He knew she wanted him to keep hitting her; she wanted him to thrash her bottom until the pain and the pleasure became one overwhelming current of sensation. So obligingly, he brought his hand down again, and then again, punctuating each blow with the same question, 'And where was the bottle?'

'In my pussy!' she cried. 'The bottle was in my pussy, and he was fucking me with it. Ralph was fucking me with the bottle. He pushed it in and out of me like a thick glass prick spraying my insides with alcohol!'

'What else did he do to you?' David positioned his solid

35

member so its swollen tip brushed her anus. She felt the contact and her buttocks clenched instinctively.

'What else did he do to you?' he repeated relentlessly.

'He fucked my ass,' she admitted in a shamed whisper.

'Like this?' He pushed until his engorged glans disappeared from view.

'Yes,' she breathed, 'like that… yes…'

He took her slowly, maintaining his control by alternately pumping hard and fast into her bottom and resting motionless deep inside her. But he could not hold an orgasm off forever, and he leaned forward to squeeze her breasts as he felt himself coming. The discomfort of being milked so firmly by her tight hole only intensified his pleasure, and he was glad she fought the urge to push back against him to feed her own pleasure. She seemed to know her enjoyment had to come solely from the knowledge that he was taking his, and from the physical and mental struggle it cost her to accommodate him as he neared his peak, and his cock grew almost unbearably thick and hard as he thrust it deeper and deeper inside her.

When he climaxed, she distinctly felt his sperm surging down his pulsing erection, and she shuddered beneath the explosive release of his tension as he fired his milky seed deep into her body. She accepted it willingly, basking in his groans and holding her position until he had emptied himself completely.

He slipped out of her, freed her wrists, and climbed onto the bed. When he was settled comfortably against the pillows, he told her to bring him a smoke and patted the mattress beside him.

She disappeared out onto the balcony, and then stepped back into the room in the process of lighting his cigarette. She handed it to him and, lighting one for herself, snuggled up beside him on the bed. 'Thank you,' she said. 'When I saw how confident you were in the restaurant, I hoped you would know what I needed.'

'Did you have any idea you were a submissive before you met Ralph?'

'No.'

'Where is he now?'

'I don't know.' There was a tinge of genuine sadness in her voice. 'After two days, he took me back to his mooring, kicked me off the boat and told me never to come back. I told him I loved him and that I'd do anything he wanted if he let me stay with him, but he said he was married.' She stubbed her cigarette out abruptly in an ashtray on the nightstand.

David slipped his hand beneath her hair, gripped the back of her neck, and pushed her face down towards his still semi-erect penis. 'Perhaps we can find you another master,' he said.

When he woke up the next day, David's clothes were folded neatly on the chaise lounge, and he was alone. He got out of bed, and discovered all his toiletries neatly laid out in the bathroom. His shaving equipment was on the shelf beneath the mirror, and a hot bath was awaiting him. He smiled remembering last night's events, but then abruptly walked back into the bedroom and checked the pockets of his trousers. All his money was still there, and his smile deepened at his good fortune. His rucksack was untouched, his possessions unmolested. It had been a wonderful night, and he considered extending his spell in Seattle.

He was returning to the bathroom to shave when a brief knock at the door was followed by his young runaway returning with breakfast.

'Good morning,' she said breezily. 'I thought you'd like to sleep in, seeing as you had such a hard night.' She had borrowed something from him after all – his brushed-cotton lumber shirt. It was all she had bothered to put on when she left the room.

David lifted the front tails of the shirt. As he suspected, she was not wearing panties. He smiled his approval, plucked up a piece of toast, and carried it into the bathroom where he ate it as he spread foaming cream around his chin and began shaving.

His new friend followed him in with the tray. She set it carefully down on the towel rack, snatched up a slice of toast for herself, and sat on the toilet lid as she devoured it.

'How's my bath?' David asked.

She extended a shapely leg and dipped a toe into the water. 'Just right.'

He stepped into the tub, and sank gratefully down into hot pink bubbles that smelled intensely of roses. When he was settled, the girl picked up his plate of scrambled eggs, sat on the edge of the bath, and proceeded to feed him.

'You never told me,' David remarked between bites.

'Told you what?'

'Your name.'

'Is it important?'

'It could be.'

'Minnie,' she said, filling his mouth with another helping of egg. 'Minnie Constance.'

'What am I going to do with you, Minnie Constance?'

'You're going to take me with you.'

It was a tempting offer, but David had felt the responsibility of control too much these past few years and he wanted some time to himself. 'Tell you what,' he said, 'if you're a very good girl, I'll take you south with me, but

38

only as far as San Francisco. Then you have to promise to go home to your mother.'

It was not the wild adventure she had hoped for, but it was something, at least. 'It's a deal,' she said eagerly. 'When do we leave?'

'Just as soon as you put some clothes on.'

With Minnie in tow, David fulfilled his dream of buying an RV, even if it was only a used one, and for the rest of the day, they drove south. They only stopped twice, at a shopping centre to pick up supplies, and at a roadhouse diner for a very late lunch.

As they pulled out of the diner's parking lot, Minnie asked him casually, 'Did you see those truckers watching me?'

'Yes. What about them?'

'They were all wondering what the deal was with us. They were taking bets on whether or not you were paying me to screw you.'

'So, what are you saying?' David kept his attention on the road.

'I'm saying you're a gentleman. I'm saying you didn't hit on me when we first met, not like most guys would have. And when I told you about Ralph fucking me in the ass and beating me, you never said anything, you just listened. It didn't bother you.' She slumped down in the seat and rested her feet on the dashboard. 'Just like it didn't bother you back there when those people were looking at us and trying to figure out what was going on between us. You just carried on as if everything was normal.'

'Everything is normal.' He was thinking of her constant chatter and how bored he already was of it.

'Except that I'm nineteen-years-old and you're old enough to be my dad. But you don't act like my dad, and those people could tell.'

'It's not a problem.'

'And that's why I like you so much,' she declared, 'because nothing's a problem for you.'

'Did you like those truckers?' he asked her abruptly.

'Not them personally, no.' She reached back into the cooler they had bought and stocked and pulled out two sodas. She knocked the tops off, and handed one to him. 'But I liked what they were thinking. It got my pussy tingling knowing they wanted me.'

'What if I had told you to go with them?'

'Well, then I would have gone with them,' she said, closing her eyes and smiling as she sipped her soda. 'I would have stripped in the parking lot if that's what you'd told me to do.'

The light was beginning to fade as David pulled off the highway, and turned up a dirt road. They had gone about two miles when the trees closed in on them. 'There's about an hour of light left,' he said. 'Get out and take your clothes off.'

She obeyed him at once.

A minute later he joined her in front of the camper, where she could feel the heat from the engine on her bare flesh. 'I'm going to cane you,' he said.

'Do you beat all the young girls you pick up?' she teased, tucking her hair behind her ear in that adorable way of hers.

'If I want to, but I keep the best beatings for girls who deserve it, and can really appreciate it.'

'Is that what you've got in your hand,' she asked, a slight tremor in her voice, 'a cane?'

'Never you mind.'

She clenched her thighs together beneath a debilitating

rush of fear and excitement.

David knew she was desperate for him to begin, but he was a master and refused to be rushed. He knew the power of denial, and the potential for increased pleasure in delaying the promised pain. The tension of her expectation aroused him as he lifted the cane, and studied it for a long moment before passing its full length slowly through his other hand. Then he brought it down in a sweeping arc that cut the air with a sinister *hiss*.

'I practiced medicine once, Minnie,' he said quietly, 'so I can tell you with some authority that we understand the function of the lungs and exactly how the kidneys work and what the pancreas does. But the mind, what is it for? I'm not referring to the brain, which enables us to put one foot in front of the other. My brain does that. Your brain does that. Our brains all share the same basic functions. My heart doesn't beat differently from yours. My lungs go in and out when I breathe, just as yours do.' He passed the cane lightly across her breasts, and flicked one of her hard little nipples with the tip. 'We have the same organs, you and I, and they behave in the same way. It's in our thoughts that we're so different from each other.'

'Yes,' she whispered, hanging on his every word even as her eyes never left the weapon in his hand.

'You see, Minnie, my brain says *beat* while your brain says *I want to be beaten*. My brain craves mastery while your brain craves submission. You long for the attention and the intensity that comes when a man's entire focus is on you and your naked body.'

She wrapped her arms around herself, and her slender, trembling figure struck him as a living exclamation point affirming the truth of his words.

'Go and stand between those two trees,' he commanded,

and then said no more as she obeyed him. He followed her, pulling a thin leather cord out of his pocket, which he quickly wrapped around one of her wrists. Then he raised her arm and tied the other end of the strap to a thick and sturdy branch. He subjected her other arm to the same treatment with the other tree, and then bound her ankles in the same way. She said nothing the whole time, but her erratic breathing spoke volumes.

Then he produced a large handkerchief, and she whimpered in fear as he blindfolded her with it. She seemed about to protest, but he abruptly gagged her with another cloth. Then he stepped back, tucked the cane under his arm, and lit a cigarette. Her flawless pale skin made him think of soft moonlight in the deepening dusk, and her splayed limbs evoked the points of a star, as if her body was the entrance to another world at the end of the long dark tunnel of trees. And the only sounds in the forest were those of the deep breaths she took through her nose in an effort to control her fear and excitement.

David enjoyed the sight of her pert breasts rising and falling before he took a long, hard drag on his cigarette, and walked up to her. The burning tip gave the soft flesh of her inner thighs a rosy glow as he pointed it up towards her pussy, and let her feel the heat.

She gasped, and shook her head desperately from side to side in protest.

He tossed the butt away, and getting a good grip on the cane, stepped slightly aside.

She felt the sting before the sound of the stroke registered. She let out a muffled scream, just as another blow landed almost directly across the mark left by the first. The pain was excruciating, and she had no way of preventing it. The gag stopped her from pleading with him to stop, and from crying out for help, and no one would have heard her anyway out here in the middle of nowhere. All she could do was hope he would be able to sense, and that he would respect, her limits. She could only pray he would remain master of himself and not abuse the absolute power he had over her in these dark and dangerous moments. She felt a third agonising stroke cut into the burning flesh of her bottom, and her excitement intensified along with her trepidation and agony.

David worked up a good sweat beating her, but he never lost control.

Minnie, however, was soon completely lost in the storm of sensations raging through her body and the emotions burning in her mind. Every time the cane sliced into her helpless flesh, her desire to be the sole focus of this man's life intensified; her longing to be the centre of his universe deepening along with the hungry heat of her pussy. What she did not realise was that with every blow his own passion became more and more fierce, increasingly animalistic and devoid of human compassion.

When the cane sliced into the back of her thighs she bit into the gag as the torment rose between her legs into her pelvis like a demonic phallus thrusting and blazing up through her body. She became aware of her stomach muscles tightening and of profound, unstoppable feelings coming alive deep inside her as another blow landed across her thighs, and then another, and another...

She lost count as her thoughts began spiralling out of control, and then a particularly cruel cut across her buttocks drove the breath clean out of her. She knew she could take no more, she had to find release or she would die, and she screamed into the gag as she came like she never had before in her life.

Chapter Three

They had been on the road for over three hours and Minnie had not said a word for at least the last one of them. Normally she was a talkative girl and David was enjoying the silence, which he would have secured for himself by gagging her again, if necessary. Most of the time he spent in Russia, he had been alone. Even when he was with Teena and Mishka, there had been little conversation between them thanks to the language barrier, which he deliberately bridged only as far as was necessary.

Several wonderfully quiet hours later they passed Lincoln City on the Pacific coast. It was a magnificent route with wonderful views of the ocean. They travelled some distance further, until he finally felt it was time for a rest and pulled up in front of a restaurant overlooking the water. The entrance was between two huge sheets of panoramic glass, and outside the diner a number of rustic tables were bolted into the sandy forecourt.

He leapt out of the truck, put his hands on his hips, and stretched. Minnie climbed out more slowly, walked around the vehicle, and rested her head lazily on his shoulder, her eyes endearingly puffy from her long nap.

'I feel so free,' she told him, 'just like that seagull.' She pointed to the large gull perched on the *Café* sign. The bird had a cheeky air about it, like all wild things that know they have the best of both worlds.

'Keep your eye on him,' David said, 'or he'll be away with the pancakes.'

Minnie chose a table near the road. Cars were few and far between, however, and it was the table closest to the sea. The air was heavy with salt, and the wind was strong.

'*Do* you want pancakes?' David asked her, preparing to walk inside and place their order.

'Please, but no syrup, it's too hot and sticky. I'll just have some butter.'

There were a few other customers in the restaurant, and it was a good fifteen minutes before David stepped back outside with their food, and saw the two campers that had formed a neat line next to his own RV. Their passengers were four young men, and they were all standing around the table talking to Minnie. She was obviously enjoying their attention, and David was pleased to see her looking so relaxed and happy with people her own age.

'Okay, guys?' he asked brightly as he set the tray on the table.

There was a moment's awkward silence.

'We were just wondering if you're staying around here,' a tall, well-built young man with curly blond hair spoke up. 'We're going surfing, and we thought your daughter might like to join us.'

At least he was polite. It was almost a pity to embarrass him. 'She's not my daughter,' David said, momentarily raising their hopes before promptly dashing them again, 'she's my partner.'

Like all good surfers, they were 'cool'. Their eyes widened even as they nodded their admiration and approval of David's sexual prowess, or his large bank account, because it had to be one or the other that attracted a girl like Minnie to him.

'Hey, why don't you both come?' the blond suggested as if he had just received a divine revelation. 'We've got a few hours of sun left, and the surf's up!'

David could see from Minnie's expression that she was desperate to accept the invitation, and he had no intention of disappointing her. 'All right,' he said.

'Excellent. Do you know where the Devil's Punchbowl is?'

'No, we're not from around here.'

The young man pointed south. 'Just keep driving that way and you can't miss it. There's a small cove near there no one goes to. You can catch a few waves, have a party, do whatever you want. Meet you two there in a couple hours?'

'Where are you going now?' Minnie asked him with a nervous edge in her voice, as if she suspected they would not show up now they knew she and David were an item.

'Off to buy the necessary supplies, sweetie; beer and food, in that order.' He laughed. 'See ya there.'

They leapt back into their vans, and boisterously honked their horns as they pulled out of the parking lot.

Minnie promptly asked David if he was sure he felt like going, and he sensed she felt guilty about wanting to be with the young men. The truth was, he did not care one way or the other. She was a lovely girl, and he was going to enjoy the sexual mileage he got out of her, but he had no qualms about her fancying boys her own age.

'I had no intention of driving south without making a few stops,' he told her. 'Just don't expect *me* to hit the surf.'

'Oh, thank you! It'll be fun, you'll see.' She smiled happily, but then suddenly looked worried again.

'What's the matter?' he asked, drenching his pancakes in maple syrup.

'I don't have a bathing suit.'

46

'You have your bra and your panties,' he reminded her. 'They'll make for a perfectly acceptable bikini, in my opinion.'

Devil's Punchbowl was only a few miles south, and they almost drove right by it. Just in time Minnie caught sight of a narrow dirt path leading off the highway. David made a sharp daredevil turn on to it that delighted his young passenger, and they wound their way down towards the cove. At the bottom, after about a few hundred yards or so, the dirt road opened onto a ridge large enough to accommodate several vehicles and, just beyond it, a narrow stretch of beach led down to the deep blue waters of the Pacific. David was no expert, but the waves did not look overly impressive. The cove was protected by tall rocks and faced due west, directly into the afternoon sun. The young men had not yet arrived.

He carried some chairs and a folding table out of the RV and set them up on the sand. 'This looks like a good spot to spend the night,' he murmured to himself. Then he said more loudly, 'Fetch me a beer, Minnie.'

She had anticipated his desire. 'Here you go.' She handed him a sweating can.

'You know,' he took a sip without bothering to thank her, 'there's something about the ocean that makes one think of freedom.'

'Like that seagull back at the diner; he was free, too.' She reached up on tiptoe to plant a soft kiss on his cheek. 'A bit like us.'

'Don't you feel as though you've got no worries at all when you're listening to the waves?'

'Yes,' she whispered, unconsciously echoing the hiss of the tide. 'When I was young we only went to the beach a few times, but I remember my mom always looked happy there, and I'd be buck naked in the sand without a care in the world.'

'Would you like to be buck naked in the sand again?'

'With all those guys around?' Her breath caught. 'Do you want me to be?'

'Yes. Get undressed.'

Even though she was a bit confused by his attitude, she did as he told her to. In less than a minute she was standing completely naked beside him, her shoes and clothes lying in a small untidy pile beside one of the RV's large tyres.

'Come inside,' David ordered, tossing his empty can away carelessly; he would make her clean everything up later.

She followed him into the camper as obediently as the puppy she reminded him of when they first met, and he grabbed her by her tiny waist to prop her up on the edge of the sink.

'What are you doing?' she asked with ill-concealed excitement.

By way of an answer, he pushed her legs wide open and sprayed several lines of shaving cream over her pubic hair. Then gently, enjoying the task, he caressed the lather into her mound and over her vulva until it expanded into soft white foam. He scooped up two little balls of it with his fingertips, and playfully decorated her nipples with them. She giggled, but fell breathlessly silent again as he picked up a razor and moved it slowly up and down over her mound. That was the easy part; shaving her labia was going to be a bit more difficult. The danger involved made him nervous and inevitably aroused him, combined as it was with her absolute faith in him and his abilities.

He began with the delicate skin between her inner thighs

and her pudenda, moving the razor slowly and carefully. Then he used the fingers of his other hand to penetrate the thick foam and smooth down the pouting lips of her sex before he brought the blade's sharp metal tongue into contact with them. 'How does that feel?' he asked her quietly.

'It feels really nice,' she murmured.

'You'll look lovely,' he assured her.

'It feels sexy,' she acknowledged.

When he was finished, he lifted her down off the sink and cleaned her up with a wet towel. She moaned as he caressed her pussy with the slightly rough terrycloth, a bit more forcefully than necessary, and made as if to slip her arms around his neck.

'Your friends are here,' he announced, stepping back out of her reach as they both heard the loud crunch of tyres outside on the rocky ridge.

She gave a little cry of mingled fear and excitement and covered her freshly shaved sex with both hands. Her mound was flushed a delicate rose colour from the caress of the razor, followed by his vigorous rubdown.

'Go get your panties,' he commanded her, 'and bring them to me.'

She ran out of the camper, and returned almost immediately. 'They didn't see me!' she panted.

'Leg up,' he instructed.

'Yo there, anyone home?' a voice called from outside.

'We'll be out in a second!' Minnie yelled.

'Now get one of my white T-shirts,' David said as he pulled her panties up her slender legs and her rosy pussy disappeared from view.

She quickly found one in his suitcase, handed it to him, and helpfully raised her arms.

'The waves won't wait!' another impatient voice warned them.

'We're coming!' The folds of David's T-shirt descending over her head muffled Minnie's cry, if not her excitement. It was much too big for her, of course, and covered half her slender thighs.

When they finally stepped outside together, the four young men were already in the ocean. Their surfboards were lying across the sand and they were playing with a ball, apparently trying to see how many times they could hit it back and forth before it landed in the water.

'Go join them,' David said when Minnie remained standing beside him looking unsure of herself. 'Go on. Have some fun.'

'What about you?'

Smiling, he glanced down at the fresh beer in his hand, and then squinted up at the sun beginning its gradual descent into the sea.

One of the boys saw her, and shouted her name as they all turned and waved, urging her to join them. She smiled at them, waved back, and ran towards the water.

David watched her racing across the sand. The strong ocean breeze blew up her T-shirt, and for a few tantalising instants her white panties were visible. Her whole body was firm, and her bottom quivered slightly as she ran and the muscles beneath her tender cheeks did their work. She sprinted through the waves breaking and ebbing on the shore, and then high-stepped her way to the edge of the group of boys, who were much taller than she was and could wade in deeper. She glanced over her shoulder at David, and smiled at him before she turned back to the game. She hit the ball when it flew her way, turning sideways to catch it, and with the sun hitting her straight on, her small breasts were clearly visible as they bounced up and down inside his T-shirt. The waves lapping against her quickly soaked the thin white cotton, which clung even more revealingly to her petite but curvaceous figure, and the young men could not help but notice.

David watched the scene with a pleasantly detached curiosity. She fit in well with the boys, who struck him as decent lads. They played together well, with no sign of the power struggles young men usually suffer from. Then a high throw Minnie had no hope of catching sent the ball plunging into the water before her. But naturally she tried to catch it, lost her balance, and vanished beneath the waves.

Just as David expected, the tall blond chap was there to help her when she surfaced. He held her steady against him while she ran her hands over her laughing face and smoothed her hair back out of her eyes. Her T-shirt was now almost completely transparent and clung to her in a way that left little to the imagination. Her breasts would be distinctly visible to the young men, and from his angle David could see the sweet ridge between her buttocks where the material had ridden up and was now deliciously trapped.

The game then got a little rougher; also a development David had anticipated. Minnie ended up in the water a lot, which kept her shirt nice and wet, and the young men took turns wrestling the ball from her.

David watched the youngsters playing for about fifteen minutes before he turned away from the water and wandered up the cliff in search of driftwood. He could cook and sleep in the RV, but he felt like lighting a fire on the beach and spending at least part of the night outside, like a castaway.

There were no rich pickings, but he managed to collect an armful of dry branches, which he piled up on the sand in front of the RV. The sun would soon be kissing the horizon and was casting a flaming path across the darkening water. He waved at Minnie, who was now perched high above the waves on one of the boys' shoulders, from which she was mock wrestling two other laughing young men, using both her arms and her legs to fight them as she laughed happily. After a few minutes she was expertly transferred onto another strong young back, and that way they all got to feel her pussy against their skin, with flesh kept away from flesh only by a skimpy pair of soaking wet panties.

This time David walked along the beach, where he found and collected bits of flotsam and jetsam, including a pair of fluorescent pink thong panties, very sporty and very sexy. Apparently this was a popular spot for lovers.

As he strolled back in the direction of the campsite he noticed the surfboards were gone, and he spotted Minnie and the boys far out in the water waiting to catch a wave. The ocean was a little too calm, but they managed a few short rides. Minnie didn't surf, of course, but she looked perfectly happy cheering her new friends on.

Smiling indulgently, David turned his full attention to building a fire. The dry wood was ablaze in seconds, and sending trails of white smoke reaching for the first few impatient stars appearing in the sky. Satisfied it would burn for some time, he then got out his recently acquired fishing rod and set off again down the beach. It only took him about forty-five minutes to land three gleaming sea bass. To the delight of the swirling seagulls, he topped and tailed the fish right there, and then threw the entrails into the sea. The birds descended in a squawking, riotous mass as the sun finally dissolved into the red water like a final drop of divine blood.

Feeling pleased with himself, he returned to the cove and stoked the fire. In the RV's tiny kitchen he then prepared the fish by stuffing them with fennel and chives and sprinkling them liberally with sea salt and pepper. While he was so engaged, the youngsters returned from their fun in the water. They had been to their campers for towels and were drying themselves off. No doubt the boys were hoping Minnie would take off her wet T-shirt and let them see what they had been surreptitiously feeling up for hours, but she disappointed them by drying her legs and her hair and then sitting down next to the fire. Her admirers would have to content themselves with watching her T-shirt dry.

David emerged from the RV, and she smiled at him joyfully. She looked stunningly innocent at that moment, which prompted him to bend over and give her a light but lingering kiss on the mouth. Her lips tasted of salt, and were as soft and succulent as the inside of a mollusc.

A stocky lad with dark hair walked back from the camper carrying a case of beer and a radio, and the festivities began in earnest.

'Oh, where did you get those?' Minnie asked when a short while later David brought out the stuffed bass.

He rolled his eyes and everyone laughed, including Minnie.

The tall blond boy's name was Paul, and he was curious about how David intended to cook the fish.

'Like this,' he said and, using a length of wood to separate the burning logs, revealed a bed of embers. He brushed those away, and exposed three flat stones he had earlier placed in the fire. He drizzled some oil over them, which sizzled appetisingly as he laid the fish across the hot rocks. Dinner was ready in a matter of minutes.

They ate the fresh bass with their fingers, and everyone agreed it was delicious. At one point, each one of the young men looked over the flames at David to nod his approval, and the older man knew it was not only his culinary skills they respected. Darkness had long since fallen; the only light came from the flames of their campfire. Outside its cosy glow, the night was an impenetrable inky black. The moon was not yet visible beyond the eastern cliffs.

'Who's up for a swim?' Paul asked suddenly.

'Swimming at night is a bit dangerous, isn't it?' Minnie replied, looking in the direction of the ocean. The rolling sound of waves unfurling against the shore and then hissing back out in the form of dangerous undertows, obviously struck her as menacing in the absolute darkness.

'Nah, just keep your eyes on the fire, and you'll be fine.'

'Let's do it!' his friends all cried in chorus.

Minnie was still hesitating when David leaned towards her. 'Live dangerously,' he whispered in her ear.

'Aren't you coming with us?' she asked anxiously.

He looked around him at the four young men waiting so intently for his answer the fire-lit air almost crackled with tension. 'I'm a little tired,' he announced. 'You go ahead.'

'But what if the flames goes out?' Minnie was still clearly not sold on the idea of a nocturnal swim.

'I won't let them,' David promised her, and once again her absolute faith in him brought his penis to attention as she leapt eagerly to her feet.

'Okay, let's do it,' she said, and they all ran whooping and cheering towards the heaving black mass of the Pacific Ocean.

David watched them disappear, and then heard their half triumphant, half shocked screams as they hit the waves. He knew the heat from the fire had warmed their flesh and would make the water feel very cold, at least at first. He smiled, threw some of the rubbish and uneaten food into the fire, and then grabbed a beer to take back to the RV.

Minnie was about fifty yards from the beach and treading water. In the glow of the fire she saw David walking back towards the camper with a beer in his hand and, suddenly, she felt very alone. There was a sprinkling of bright and energetic stars above her, and when she turned her back on the fire, it was impossible for her to tell where the ocean ended and the sky began. It was a spooky experience that tightened her stomach muscles as she experienced that rush of excitement mingled with danger she was becoming familiar with, and her fear brought with it a heightened sense of awareness. Her eyes stared intently into the darkness trying to spot anything unusual, anything that might prove a threat to her vulnerable young flesh, and she shuddered at the thought of a shark swimming invisibly and silently around her, ready to sink its fatally sharp teeth into her defenceless body. Her nerves prickling with primeval instincts of self-preservation, she turned back in the direction of the RV, and saw a tiny red flash inside it. David was sitting in the driver's seat smoking a cigarette, and the knowledge that he was looking her way made her feel irrationally safe. He was giving her some freedom, but he was still there to protect her… and in return, he was expecting to be entertained…

The water suddenly exploded beside her, but her scream was cut off as an irresistible force pulled her under. She fought her way to the surface, and was greeted by a ring of young men surrounding her very much like a group of hungry sharks. She took a deep breath to yell out David's name, but Paul's mouth cut off her cry. He tongued her deeply before shoving her towards Gary, who reluctantly relinquished her to Steve, after which Darren finally got his turn.

'Bastards!' she gasped.

Four strong hands pressed down on her head, and she went under again. When they finally let her come up for air she barely had time to catch her breath before another eager tongue slipped between her lips. They passed her around a second time, subjecting her to hungry kisses that might have been mistaken for desperate efforts at mouth-to-mouth resuscitation except for the hands leisurely fondling her breasts. The cold water had stiffened her nipples and made them especially sensitive to being tweaked and pulled and rubbed, and her breasts rose and fell swiftly in an effort to escape all this attention while she also kept struggling to catch her breath. Then she went under again, only this time it was because someone was tugging on her panties, and she was not allowed to resurface until she stopped fighting to keep them on. They slipped down her legs as if ripped off her by a powerful undertow, and this time a hand slipped between her thighs as a fat and salty tongue filled her mouth.

'Well *fuck* me,' Gary said in wonder, 'her pussy's shaved smooth as can be!'

Beneath the water, a school of hungry hands reached for her sex.

Whimpering, Minnie went the way of all outnumbered prey since the beginning of time, and surrendered. The young men became increasingly aggressive the more turned on they got, and her only defence was not to fight them. She was not even sure she wanted to, really, or maybe her mind was simply overloaded by the myriad of sensations demanding its attention. Her bottom, her breasts and her pussy were all being squeezed and caressed at once, and she felt the unmistakable hardness of erect cocks nudging her belly and her lower back. They were pulling her closer to the beach while they kept passing her around between them, and as each kiss grew longer and more insistent, she felt urgent thrusts from expectant hips demanding to mount her. Someone had to take charge.

'Take her up to the beach,' Paul ordered. 'We'll fuck her in front of her old man's camper so he can watch.'

David was waiting patiently. He had just lit another cigarette when five half naked bodies ran into the halo of firelight. Minnie was still wearing her T-shirt, but it had hiked up around her waist and he could see her panties were missing. Gary was leading her by the hand, and he spread himself out on the sand in front of her and pulled her down on top of him. Immediately four hands tugged the T-shirt up over her head, and David got a tantalising glimpse of her delicate body before it was surrounded like a deer by a pack of strong young lions beginning to feast on her.

He remained a not entirely passive observer in the darkness of the RV. He had removed his clothes and was sitting naked in the driver's seat, his penis erect and swollen and pressing insistently against his belly. He took it in his hand and slowly began stroking it. When his orgasm threatened, he pulled on his cigarette and the smoke helped relax him enough to continue watching the scene unfolding out on the sand in the flames' passionately flickering spotlight.

Gary was still lying on his back, and Minnie was sucking his cock while offering her bottom up to Paul. Steve and Darren knelt on either side of her, waiting their turn. Judging by the way she kept lifting her face off Gary's rod and throwing her head back, Paul's penis was too big and too hard for her tight little arse, but he kept thrusting it in and out of her cheeks' smooth divide. Then suddenly she opened her eyes, and looked straight up at the glowing tip of David's cigarette. She knew then that he was watching her, and everything was all right, because this was what he wanted, and she was pleasing him. Her face sank down over Gary's cock again, and her head bobbed efficiently up and down as Paul pumped himself in and out of her buttocks with increasing urgency. He kept a firm grip on her hips as he banged her, and when Gary gripped her head to run it up and down his prick at his own pace, it left Minnie's hands free to reach up and grip the two cocks waiting impatiently to enter her. It was a totally sluttish, and yet also strangely graceful gesture.

From his front row seat in the RV, David watched the scene playing silently in front of him whilst stroking his erection, and groaned out loud as he saw Paul's body stiffen after one last forceful lunge that signalled his ejaculation. Steve immediately took his place behind the girl when Paul pulled out of her, and David groaned again as the young man ignored her semen-slick sphincter and thrust straight into her pussy's soft clutches. Steve thrashed in and out of her in a way that made it clear he had waited too long for the pleasure. Hanging his head in mingled relief and shame, he came almost at once. Darren impatiently took his place, and punctuated each of his energetic thrusts with a hard slap from his open palm across her bottom as it quivered beneath his pumping hips.

David could guess the effect the spanking was having on her, and his cockhead swelled in anticipation of her reaction. He did not have long to wait, and Minnie's scream as she climaxed was clearly audible to him even through the thick glass of the windshield. His grip on himself tightened as he watched an orgasm sweep through her slender young body with all the force of the tide breaking behind her. With

Gary's cock buried in her mouth, she bucked wildly back against Darren's hips, milking the spunk out of his pulsing cock and, unknown to her, out of David's as well.

The thick jet of his sperm sprayed the dashboard, and trickled slowly down the face of the speedometer. But whereas he had arrived at the point of perfect relaxation, the boys were far from finished with Minnie.

She was lying on her back now. Gary was kneeling between her legs, and Paul was crouched behind her. Steve and Darren were positioned at her shoulders, and David watched with interest as they reached down over her body, and pulled her ankles up over her head. The last thing he saw before he got up and went to bed was Gary forcing his thick dick into her invitingly proffered bottom.

David woke up first, and kissed Minnie lightly on the cheek. 'Time for breakfast,' he whispered. 'You must be starving after all the exercise you got last night.'

She murmured a sleepy protest, and turned over on her side.

He pulled back one of the curtains to look outside. It was raining hard, and the two other RVs were gone.

The coast looked a desolate place in the rain. The gentle waves of the previous day had turned into white-capped mountains, and the wind drove a blinding spray across the highway.

Minnie turned up the heater. 'I love this weather,' she sighed happily.

'It's nice,' David agreed, 'but it makes driving rather difficult.'

'Should we stop?'

'We've got a long way to go.'

'So, what's the rush? Pull over for a minute and I'll make us some coffee.'

David used the break to stretch his legs out on the sofa. Minnie brought over their coffee, and sat down beside him.

For several minutes neither one of them said a word as they sipped their coffee, gazing out at the rain swept scene.

'Listen to that…' she broke their silence. 'I love that sound.' She glanced up at the roof and cocked her head in that puppyish way that delighted David.

He smiled at her almost affectionately, and reached for his cigarettes. 'Reminds me of family holidays in Llandudno,' he remarked.

She accepted a cigarette. 'Back home?'

He nodded, and studied a seagull hungrily patrolling the beach while being mercilessly buffeted by the wind.

'Do you miss it?' she asked tentatively.

'Only when the weather's like this.' He thought about home for a while before adding, 'But the longer you stay away, the easier it is to forget; your friends, your family, everything.'

'Well, you've got me now.'

'For a while.' He kissed her gently on the lips.

'For always,' she whispered earnestly. 'I can look after you. I'll do whatever you want. You know I will. You saw me last night, I—'

'I saw a young girl having a lot of fun with some young men, and she looked very happy indeed.'

'She was, but she's much happier here now with you.'

'We'll have many more good times before we have to worry about you going back home, Minnie, I promise.' He lifted her skirt, and was disappointed to observe that she was wearing a skimpy pair of panties.

'I shaved in the shower this morning,' she told him proudly. 'Would you like to see?'

'Mm,' he murmured, smiling.

She left her cigarette burning in the ashtray as she stood up, pushed her panties down, and stepped out of them.

He patted the table in front of him.

She climbed up on it and sat cross-legged before him holding her skirt up around her waist, revealing a beautifully smooth mound cleaved by a neat line. She did not have full and well-defined sex lips; they were more like two slender petals on either side of her pussy's dark heart. David idly caressed the inside of one of her thighs and blew smoke over her pudenda.

'Oh,' she moaned, shivering, 'that's nice.'

'I like it like this,' he said. 'A shaved pussy looks so nice and neat and clean.'

Minnie hiked her skirt up even higher, and gazed down at herself. Then she retrieved her cigarette, took a drag, and blew the smoke over her smooth mound. 'When I was little, I was so desperate for my beaver to start growing,' she mused. 'Me and my girlfriends used to examine each other to see if we could spot any tiny hairs sprouting, and now look at me, I've shaved it all off.'

Casually, he slipped two fingers up inside her. She tossed her head back and let out a long, low moan of pleasure.

He finger-fucked her slowly, enjoying the control he possessed over the young beauty.

Panting, her eyes closed, she began grinding herself against his fingers, desperately trying to get him to rub her clitoris with the heel of his hand.

'Get up on your knees and turn around,' he instructed, pulling his fingers out of her clinging slickness. The fresh scent of her pleasure was discernable through the stale smell of cigarette smoke.

She did as she was told, positioning herself on the table with her bottom facing him, her skirt still bunched up around her waist. She did not have an ounce of fat on her, but her figure was still appealingly curvaceous.

David leaned forward and touched her tightly puckered little arsehole with the tip of his tongue. Then he lifted her soft cheeks in both his hands, and licked each one in turn like scoops of vanilla ice cream, breathing in the clean scent of her freshly washed skin, and the deeper, almost syrupy odour of her arousal. Then he began finger-fucking her pussy again, deliberately taking his time as he pushed two digits up inside her as deeply as they would go, and then pulled them all the way out again to teasingly caress her sex lips with his fingertips.

When his fingers were deep inside her she rocked back and forth on his hand, whimpering as her swelling clit sought his elusive caress. He seemed to be deliberately tormenting her by ignoring it, and a slight sheen of perspiration broke out on her skin from the desperate effort she was making to come; to harvest all the delicious sensations his touch was blooming inside her in the form of a hot and juicy and utterly gratifying climax.

He pulled his fingers out of her pussy, stood up, and walked around the small table to face her.

She looked up at him, her dark eyes wide with a hunger that pleaded to be fed, and she finally saw him preparing her meal as he unbuckled his belt. But he did not unzip his pants. He simply pulled his belt off and wrapped it around his hand several times, leaving just enough of the strap hanging from his fist to beat her with. She moaned as he held it up in front of her face. His expression was unreadable, but she instinctively knew what he wanted from her. Closing her eyes, she puckered her lips and dutifully kissed the cool, firm leather. And the thought that she was about to feel the belt's cruel cut against her defenceless skin almost brought her to orgasm without her having to touch herself. The stab of fear and pleasure she experienced knowing he was about to be cruel and whip her affected her clitoris almost as intensely as an actual physical pressure. Then he stepped around behind her again and she fell forward onto her hands, weak and breathless with excitement.

His first blow was a feint, a whisper-light caress across her bottom, and it nearly made her delirious with anticipation as she kept her buttocks thrust obediently up in the air for him. 'Oh, God, beat me,' she begged, 'please!'

A rush of blood stretched David's cock almost to bursting. His instinct was to sink his erection between her pert cheeks and ride her for all she was worth. But he resisted his primeval programming for a while in favour of the infinitely more subtle pleasures of the mind. He knew she was already well into a powerfully arousing world of her own making, in which his will was God, and the power he had over her turned her on like a divine revelation. It was a world in which the law of gravity was reduced to the pressure of her own fingertips against her clitoris, and the feel of a belt burning across her flesh was all she would ever need to know of heaven and hell.

'Oh, God, please use me,' she gasped. 'You can do anything you want to me – *anything*. You can—' Her plea turned into a sharp cry as he answered her prayer and landed the belt viciously in the tender space between her rounded cheeks and slender thighs. Then he struck her again just a little higher, on the intensely sensitive skin at the base of her buttocks, which quivered beautifully as the leather sliced into them. She screamed, and her entire body tensed when an orgasm lanced up through her body and pulled her head back as if an invisible force was riding her.

A full fifteen minutes later, waves of pleasure were still surging up between her parted thighs. David had turned her over onto her back, and subjected her to another searing climax simply by slapping the belt lightly across her pussy, just barely catching her clit with the firm leather, but it was enough to send her over the edge again, and then again.

Now she was still lying there with her skirt hiked up around her waist as they both smoked another cigarette. She was gazing up at the ceiling, lost in her own world as she idly played with herself, and he slowly stroked his rigid cock, watching her.

'I love it when you beat me,' she said dreamily. 'You wanted me to fuck those guys, didn't you? You're not punishing me for that now, are you?'

'No, I'm not, but you also wanted it.'

'Yes, I did,' she admitted. 'Yet it wasn't right, was it? It's not right to let a bunch of guys do whatever they want to you, especially after you just met them. I knew they were only using me, but I didn't care because I knew I had your permission. And that's what made it so naughty, knowing it was what you wanted, for all of them to fuck me like that even though it was wrong. If you hadn't been there, and if I hadn't been doing it to please you, it wouldn't have been the same. I think I would have felt cheap, and scared. But you *were* there, so I didn't have to be scared, and I felt wicked and beautiful, not cheap, because I was obeying you and doing what you wanted. I did it just to please you.'

'You did it just to please me,' he echoed quietly, drawing thoughtfully on his cigarette and then blowing the warm dry smoke straight into her hot wet pussy.

'Yes,' she answered fervently. 'I never want to stop pleasing you because you understand me.'

'Have you learned anything in the time we've been together, Minnie?'

'Oh yes, I've learned to *love* cock,' she confessed bluntly. 'I've learned to love what a man can make me feel.'

'And what else?'

She thought about it for some time. 'I've learned to be myself,' she said at last. 'I've learned not to be afraid of my own feelings because some people might think they're strange.'

'That's good.'

'I think,' she put out her cigarette abruptly and slid off the table, 'I'm going to be myself from now on.' She made as if to straddle him.

'Naked,' he said firmly.

She promptly pushed off her wrinkled skirt, and then stood motionless before him so he could inspect her. She was a beautiful young specimen, and totally willing to please. He was more than ready for her, and with a simple nod of his head, he commanded her to mount him. She responded by flinging her leg over his thighs, and guiding his stiff cock into her eager slot.

'Easy,' he murmured, 'put it in slowly.'

She had trouble obeying him she was so anxious to feel his prick sliding into her, but she managed to take her time stabbing herself with him, and when she finally felt him sinking into her, she moaned in ecstasy and closed her eyes.

'Now move slowly,' he instructed her, 'and let me enjoy you.'

Resisting the urge to bounce wildly up and down on his shaft, she forced herself to relax and slide her clinging pussy slowly up and down his full length while he fondled her breasts and sucked gently on her nipples. Then he sat back and caressed her toned flesh, following the curves of her waist as it flared gently out to her hips. He slipped a finger into her mouth, and let her suck on it passionately before he pulled it out, reached down behind her, and thrust it up into her bottom.

She squirmed and moaned and her vaginal muscles gripped his rigid penis even harder as the electric current of yet another climax began spreading through her pelvis. It was a nice feeling for him, and he got her to milk his cock even harder with her pussy by finger-fucking her arse, pushing his invading digit in deep to feel her squeeze his prick in response. He controlled her pleasure by manipulating all her senses while satisfying all of his own. He licked and tasted her skin, smelled the scent of her arousal, listened to her moans, and admired her body riding up and down his erection as her cunt squeezed him lovingly, and more and more urgently.

'You know, of course,' he began quietly, feeling the moment had come for him to drop the bomb, 'that you have to go home soon.'

'What?' she gasped. 'But you said—'

'I'm sorry,' he cut her off, 'but you said you would do anything I told you to do, and very soon I'm going to tell you to go home, and you're going to obey me.'

Tears sprang into her eyes, and her bottom lip trembled as she swallowed her protests.

'But we still have some time left together,' he relented, 'so don't cry.'

'Then I want the time we have left to be perfect,' she said fervently.

'I'm going to test you,' he warned.

'How?' She continued to ride him slowly, not allowing

his pleasure to overflow so she could keep his cock solidly embedded inside her for as long as possible.

'I want you to go away for two nights,' he informed her, 'so I can see how you react when I'm not around. You'll be with someone else, and they'll have the same power over you that I do.'

'But—'

'I want you to be another man's slave for two nights,' he stated bluntly.

'Yes, master,' she said softly, lowering her eyes, 'whatever you want. When do you—?'

'Tonight. I'll take you to a truck stop on the highway, and you'll hitch a ride with one of the drivers.'

She gasped in pleasure as his forceful tone mingled with the experience of his rock-hard penis sliding in and out of her pussy, which yielded to him and clung to him in the way all her feelings seemed to.

'I'll choose the driver, and then you'll go with him and make sure he's pleased with you... very pleased with you. Do you understand?'

She bit her lip and nodded, her cheeks flushing with shame at how much the thought excited her, and because she was very close to coming again.

'This is to be part of your training, Minnie. It will teach you that pleasure can be experienced with just about anyone if you're willing to give something of yourself, or in this case, *all* of yourself.' He gripped her hips and began sliding her swiftly up and down his pulsing erection. 'You're to hold nothing back from this man. You're to give him everything he wants, no matter what it is.'

'Yes, master,' she cried, 'yes... oh yes...' She wrapped her arms around his neck as she climaxed, trembling against him as he ejaculated deep inside her, depositing his seed along with his commands in what felt like the very core of her being.

Chapter Four

The rain continued for most of the day, during which they sat in the back of the RV enjoying the grand spectacle of thunderstorms playing themselves out across the western sky. Then they ate some dinner, and set off through a murky twilight in search of a truck stop.

Minnie grew increasingly apprehensive. All day she had been hoping David had only been saying all that about her having to be another man's slave for two nights in order to turn himself on as he fucked her. But when a tacky red-and-blue neon sign lit up the drizzling dusk and he turned off the highway towards it, her heart skipped a beat when she realised he had meant it all.

Her stomach knotted when she saw two long rows of trucks parked neatly behind each other to form a strangely brooding metal caravan.

David pulled up in front of the diner, and she managed to flash him a smile as she opened her door and followed him out into the cool night. The knocking sounds coming from inside the RV's hood seemed unusually loud to her, and she was grateful for the engine's warmth as she shivered and hugged herself. Then David took her arm and she leaned gratefully against him, somehow controlling the urge to hug him and cling to him as tenaciously as a terrified kitten.

'Be brave,' he said simply, and led her inside.

The diner was not much brighter than the damp and gloomy evening outside. Neon beer signs and a handful of pinball machines supplied most of the illumination, along with three dark-green lamps hanging from the ceiling above three pool tables. No one seemed to notice them walk in, which was not surprising considering the thick mist of cigarette smoke.

They went and sat on two high stools at the bar, close to a jukebox. A quick glance told David the songs inside it were all at least fifteen-years-old. A gaunt biker-type wearing a sleeveless denim vest over black leathers pants exchanged a couple of dimes for a few minutes of pounding heavy metal. He gave Minnie's face a rather blank stare, before checking out her legs in the short denim cut-offs David had provided for her by taking a knife to her jeans. The man mumbled something about her nice tight ass, and ambled back to his pool game.

David signalled the barman, and ordered two beers. The bottles arrived a minute later, and he touched Minnie's elbow to indicate she should follow him to a booth. She was unusually quiet, and he left her to her thoughts to go write his name on a board, putting himself in line for a game of pool. The group of bikers eyed him with amusement and reluctant admiration; not many middle-aged men had balls enough to ignore their unsavoury reputation and take them on at their own game.

In the next couple of hours David won some and lost a few others. The bikers liked his accent, which pegged him as an outsider just like them, and it was not long before they were buying him beers.

'Does the lady want another drink?' asked the jukebox patron, the question put to David, not Minnie. 'I'd sure like to buy her one.'

'I'm sure she does,' her master said, using this opportunity to set his plan in motion. 'She's hitching a ride south, and if she didn't have the money to buy herself a bus ticket, then she probably doesn't have enough to buy herself another beer.'

Within moments a fresh bottle was placed at her elbow. 'How far do you wanna go, little lady?' her rough admirer asked her, almost politely.

David sank the blue ball and picked up his beer. 'I've already taken her all the way,' he answered for her. 'Now I've just got to unload her.'

Grinning, the biker studied David intently for a moment. The Englishman was an enigma to him. He was travelling the West coast alone, he was not afraid to mix with bikers, and he had obviously sampled the charms of a lovely young American girl.

'I get your drift, buddy,' he said finally, and turned his attention back to Minnie. 'Is your friend right? You looking to work your way south?' He emphasised the word 'work', and spoke loudly enough that his friends interrupted their game to wait expectantly for her reply.

'I'm going south, yes,' she said quietly while looking sweetly up into his bloodshot eyes with her own big brown ones, 'the easiest way possible.' She was hopelessly confused. David had said she was to spend the next two nights with a trucker, and yet he appeared to be giving her away to a bunch of bikers. Yet she had no choice but to go along with whatever he had planned for her. She could only assume he had changed his mind.

David motioned for her to join the action by inclining his head towards the pool table, and despite her anxiety, Minnie announced she wanted to play, and slipped out of the booth.

'Let the lady through,' her admirer said loudly, 'she wants to play with us.'

The rough-and-tumble group hooted their approval, and the atmosphere lifted almost miraculously. Minnie immediately became the centre of attention, and true to her trusting and fun-loving nature she relished every minute of it. She had never played pool before in her life, but that certainly did not stop her from trying to learn right then and there, and her suitor, whose name turned out to be Bobby, was more than happy to teach her by helping her line up her shots. Standing behind her, he pressed himself tightly up against her and bent her over the table so his hard crotch dug into her soft bottom.

David left his slave to enjoy all the attention she was getting, and satisfied his curiosity about the bikers by talking to each one of them in turn. He discovered they were a local chapter about twenty strong, and that most of them worked as mechanics. By chatting with the bartender, he also learned the bikers had a lodge about five miles up the road they used for wild parties, and just to crash in.

'They call it the Gang Bang Ranch, and the way your friend's behaving, I'm pretty sure she's gonna find out why.'

Minnie was bent over the table lining up a shot and Bobby was leaning into her. He had his hand resting alongside hers on the pool table as he showed her how to make a bridge with her fingers over the cue, and after she took the shot, her caressed her arm as they both straightened up. Then he boldly cupped one of her breasts and kissed the side of her neck.

David's cock reacted to the sight, and his brain followed it as he scanned the diner. He noticed a dozen or so truckers looking enviously at the bikers, who had taken possession of Minnie. She was one of the few females in the bar, and the only truly attractive one. Little did these drivers know how lucky one of them had almost gotten tonight, but it was not to be. David had learned how to adapt to changing circumstance, and this was such an occasion. He began pondering the possibilities of Gang Bang Ranch, and decided Minnie should pay it a visit.

When Bobby disappeared into the lavatory, David took Minnie another bottle of beer and drew her aside. 'Be yourself,' he told her firmly.

'Where are you going?' she asked in alarm.

'Not far, don't worry. Just go with the flow, as they say, and live the experience. I'll be watching you the whole time, I promise.'

'I don't know what you mean,' she protested weakly. 'I—'

'Just do as I say, and be yourself.'

Bobby stepped back out into the bar, and saw David and Minnie talking together. He liked the Englishman, but he was not going to tolerate anyone outside the chapter moving in on what he now considered his property. He strode purposefully up to the furtively whispering pair.

'Just saying goodbye,' David explained, and squeezed her arm as he began walking away. 'I'm sure you'll be all right here, Minnie. One of these guys will give you a lift.'

Somehow she managed to restrain herself; she did not cling to him and beg him not to go, although she longed to do so. She did not know if she was just being paranoid, but suddenly all eyes in the diner seemed to be focused not just on her, but very specifically on her pussy, as if lustful thoughts had the power to burn away the denim concealing it. Music throbbed loudly from the jukebox and the pinball machines chimed, yet all sounds seemed muffled compared to how loudly her own heart was beating as all the energy in the room seemed to concentrate itself in one place – her. She felt almost sick with anxiety as David walked out of the diner, and left her alone with dozens of rough and horny men.

She desperately remembered his promise: 'I'll be watching you the whole time'. It made her feel a little safer as she glanced around her. Bikers and truck drivers were as far from the clean-cut college kids she had enjoyed on the beach the previous night as she could possibly get. These men were older, and meaner. Then she saw the way Bobby was looking at her as he bent over the table to take a shot.

Doing her best to look relaxed and not give away the scent of her fear to this pack of human wolves, she walked up to him. 'What pocket you aiming for?' she asked him sweetly.

David sat in the RV for a while to make sure Minnie did not bolt. He need not have worried. It was dark outside and the activity in the diner was visible through the misted glass. She was drinking and playing pool and swaying to the music as though she felt perfectly at home. Occasionally a hand would graze her bottom, or one of the men would pull her playfully down onto his lap, but that was all, for now. No doubt they were saving the real action for Gang Bang Ranch, and he reckoned he had about an hour to find it before they took her there.

The bartender's directions proved to be spot-on. David had prepared a story in case there were other bikers at the ranch. He would say he had become lost looking for Coquille, which his map told him was a few miles further south.

As he turned onto the dirt road the bartender had indicated, he kept an eye out for a good place to hide the RV. He was lucky and found a clearing about a half-mile from the house. His vehicle was now invisible from the road, and there was enough space for him to turn it around and park it facing in the right direction for a quick getaway.

He got out and in complete darkness made his way carefully between trees and undergrowth that had not been cut back in years, if ever, and grew almost right up to the building. 'Ranch' proved to be a rather grandiose term for a two-storey wooden-frame house. It was, however, a good-sized lot, with a large veranda running around the entire bottom floor.

There were three bikes parked out front – all Harley Davidson's. They were all polished until they gleamed in the faint starlight visible above the trees, and in top condition, which was more than could be said for their unkempt, and often overweight, owners.

David was distracted from his admiration of the bikes by noises coming from inside the house. The room closest to where he stood was lit by a couple of lamps partially obscured by furniture. As he watched, a tall silhouette approached the French doors, pushed one open and stepped out onto the veranda. The man was smoking the remnants of what looked like a thin cigar, which he finished off and tossed carelessly into the bushes.

A well-stacked girl in a black leather miniskirt and a white lace bra strolled unsteadily out of the house behind him. She was also wearing a pair of knee-high leather boots with tall thin heels. She was sipping a beer, and by the way she walked it was obvious it was not her first. There was just enough light for David to make out that she was a striking girl with a tangle of jet-black curls and distinctive features; high cheekbones and a full, pouting mouth.

She fell into the porch swing, and began rocking back and forth in a sultry parody of a naïve country girl sipping lemonade. Her companion turned towards her, and they laughed when he joined her on the swing and set it into violent motion by kicking against the veranda rail with his thick leather boot. He then slipped his large hand beneath her hair, gripped the back of her neck, and shoved her face down into his lap. He took her beer from her so she could use her hands to open his pants, and sipped it contentedly as she dutifully sucked him.

David crouched down behind some bushes to wait for Minnie's arrival as he enjoyed the scene on the porch. A moment later another biker emerged from the house. They seemed to grow them big in this part of the world; the new arrival was also tall and stocky and boasted a thick beard. He joined David as a spectator, leaning against the rail to swig his beer while casually assessing the girl's oral skills.

The pulsing growl of approaching motorcycles rent the still night air, and everyone looked their way, including David, who peered down the lane and saw the beams of several bikes lancing through the trees. The first rider to come into view was Bobby, and perched behind him on the seat, her arms wrapped around his chest and her hair streaming behind her, was Minnie. There were three other riders, and they all appeared to be in high spirits. Instead of parking straightaway, they rode around and around in a tight circle for a minute, revving their engines while whooping and shouting. And Minnie – who David could tell was quite drunk – contributed to this mechanical powwow with Banshee-like shrieks of her own.

Several times a high-intensity headlight swept over David's position behind the bushes, but no one noticed the face peering out at them from between the branches. When the engines were finally cut, the profound silence that followed was almost unnerving. Then a third biker emerged from the house and tossed a six-pack of beer at Bobby, who caught it, took a can for himself, and passed it on.

The girl on the swing had stopped blowing her partner to

greet the new arrivals. She managed not to trip as she swayed down the veranda steps in her spiky heels, and walked straight up to Bobby.

'Hey, Angel,' he said fondly.

Angel was staring at Minnie. 'Who's this cute little thing?'

'We brought you a playmate. Her name's Minnie.'

'Hi, there.' Angel smiled and caressed Minnie's cheek as though she was a life-sized doll that was all hers now. 'You're a pretty little thing.'

'Thank you.' Minnie smiled back. She had enjoyed the older girl's touch; it was soft and cool and strangely sensual. Angel looked extremely sexy to her with her tousled dark hair, and her white bra straining to contain enviably full breasts. She seemed very sure of herself, and Minnie admired that. There was also something intense about her face that made it impossible for her to look away.

'Ever been with another girl, baby?' Angel came directly to the point.

Minnie shook her head.

'Think you'd like it? The boys love a good show.'

Minnie's response was to let Angel lead her up the steps. The bikers followed them, talking and laughing in anticipation.

David changed his position in order to see what was happening in the house. He had no intention of missing any of the action.

Minnie was taken to a large room, the bare walls of which were lined with overstuffed armchairs and sofas. A log fire crackled angrily in the hearth, its red glow blending luridly with an assortment of coloured lights – green, blue, purple and orange. The space was a psychedelic nightmare, and a

77

heavy metal CD was playing.

Angel turned to Minnie, and guided her head into her cleavage in a parody of maternal affection as the men settled down around them, resting heavy, oil-stained boots on ripped cushions, and balancing cans of beer on wooden armrests pockmarked with holes from the tips of burning cigarettes.

Watching through the window from outside, David was surprised at Minnie's response to Angel's overtures. She cupped the other woman's heavy breasts almost hungrily, and kissed her right back. Smiling, Angel pulled Minnie's shirt off over her head, and exposed her lovely delicate bosom to the room. The bikers cheered the sight, and they went on cheering every kiss and every caress the two girls gave each other. Their roars of approval were clearly audible over the pounding music, especially when Angel removed her own bra. Her breasts were large and firm, and her dark, erect nipples were just begging to be sucked.

She popped the first button on Minnie's denim cut-offs, and revealed a tantalising glimpse of white panties. The tension was rising, and then Minnie surprised David again by dancing away from the other woman in rhythm with the music as she continued unbuttoning her shorts. She positioned herself in front of a couch full of bikers, turned around, and pointed her cute bottom straight at them. Then she hooked her thumbs into her shorts and began pushing them down. The cheering died away as her captive audience leaned forward, eager to catch the first glimpse of her pussy.

When both her shorts and her panties passed over the beginning of the valley between her cheeks, the men all seemed to hold their breath, and David saw a number of them swallow hard in anticipation of the sight to come as they adjusted cocks swelling uncomfortably inside leather pants and jeans.

Bobby was closest to Minnie, and consequently had the best view. She wriggled her buttocks in his face, and slowly pushed her shorts and panties all the way down her shapely legs.

'Just look at that,' Bobby said in wonder, 'she's as smooth as a baby!'

'Hey, Angel, get your snatch alongside the kid's,' another voice demanded. The gruff tones emanated from a middle-aged man with a scar that ran from one cheek to the other across his nose. The angry pink line split his face in half, and had not done much to improve his personality. 'Come on, bitch,' he said, standing up impatiently. 'Get your ass over here. I just can't believe two women can have such different cunts.'

Even as Angel obediently approached the couch, Bobby was pulling Minnie down to her knees and positioning her facedown over it.

'You too, bitch,' scar-face hissed, and a younger, clean-shaven man stepped in when he grabbed Angel's arm with the intention of forcing her down beside Minnie.

'Take it easy, man,' he urged. 'Chill, will you, Jake? Everyone's having a good time here.'

Jake turned to face him, but kept a possessive grip on Angel's arm. 'No, *you* fucking chill out, man. There's plenty here for everyone, just so long as me and Bobby go first. I ain't sticking my dick up no creamed hole after you.'

The younger biker glanced nervously around the room, but no one caught his eye. It was chapter rules – the main men went first.

Angel was forced alongside Minnie, and her skirt hiked up to her waist. She was accustomed to being treated this way, and she rested her cheek placidly against the threadbare cushion. There was always an element of fear living at the Ranch with so many men having free access to her all the time, but she thrived on it. She loved living outside the law and seeing the nervous looks people gave them when they hit the towns in roaring droves. She enjoyed watching the women's faces most of all. They all pretended to look shocked as she rode through the main street on the back of a hog, her long legs parted around the one-hundred-and-twenty horsepower engine thumping between her thighs. The women in their flower-print dresses would hurry their children inside, but Angel could see it in their eyes that they fantasised about sitting on a powerful machine with their arms wrapped around a hard and uncompromising man.

Jake grabbed hold of Angel's panties and ripped them off. There was no accompanying cheer; every man in the room had fucked her before, and more than once. Jake looked across at the new girl.

Minnie was gasping beneath every violent lunge of Bobby's big cock into her pussy's tight slot.

Grumbling to himself, Jake plunged three of his fingers roughly into Angel's familiar, and therefore less exciting, cunt. She yelped beneath the rough and sudden penetration. Then he took his position kneeling behind her, and pulling his fingers out, thrust his dick home without further ceremony.

Meanwhile, Bobby was already reaching his peak inside Minnie, and as he ejaculated with a primal roar, both her mind and her body screamed for more. The moment she felt his disappointingly spent penis slip out of her, she wriggled her bottom invitingly, hungrily luring another erection her way.

She did not have long to wait, and she deliberately

refrained from looking over her shoulder to see who took her next. She had no desire to know if he was good looking and if she fancied him. It did not matter; she just needed to feel a big hard penis pumping away inside her. She did, however, turn her head to look at Angel. The other girl was moaning as Jake banged her, and as their eyes met, Angel and Minnie recognised themselves in each other. They smiled, and closed their eyes again.

It was the longest, most aggressive and most enjoyable train yet for Minnie. Every single one of the bikers had his turn with her, and some also did Angel. The girls were fucked on the floor, on the furniture, against the wall, and even bent over the railing out on the veranda. They were ridden doggie style and every other style, and both their sphincters were stretched wide when the gangbang finally petered to an end.

In between having all their available orifices filled and selfishly used, Angel and Minnie caressed each other lovingly, passing their soft hands gently and soothingly over each other's bodies, marvelling at how different they were and aroused by the contrast. Then afterwards, like athletes warming down after a major event, the girls eased each other down from a state of high sexual intensity to a peaceful plateau of gentle, relaxing sensations.

By now, all the bikers were either asleep or too exhausted to appreciate the display of girl-to-girl affection. David, however, was very much enjoying it from his hiding place outside.

The girls were so similar in mind and so different in body. Minnie, with her delicate breasts and shaved pussy, her tiny waist and innocent face, looked almost fragile against the wild-haired, voluptuous Angel. Both girls were laying on their sides now, their limbs entwined. They caressed each other occasionally, just often enough to keep sensations flickering through their overwhelmed bodies, but eventually they, too, fell asleep.

David had climaxed several times, and now he sneaked around the side of the house to smoke a cigarette and collect his thoughts as well as his strength. He glanced at his watch, using the light from his cigarette. It was almost four o'clock in the morning. The bikers had been fucking Minnie and Angel for nearly three hours. If they had been riding their bikes instead of the girls, they could have made it to Portland, and back. What David had not reckoned on at the roadhouse was just how many bikers lived at Gangbang Ranch. Getting Minnie out of there presented a serious problem. She was now the chapter's property, and he doubted they would give her up so easily.

He returned to his position in the bushes in front of the French doors. All was quiet inside. Minnie and Angel had turned away from each other as they slept, which was good; at least he didn't have to worry about untangling them.

He sucked in a deep breath, heaved himself over the railing onto the veranda, and stepped silently into the room. If it had not been for the loud snoring coming from some of the men, he might have been in some perversely enchanted kingdom where a spell had been cast over the whole leather-clad court, a spell that could be broken only by his, the prince's, kiss on Minnie's softly smiling lips. Except that he had no desire to wake anyone up.

A loose floorboard creaked beneath him, but the exhausted chapter slumbered on. He stepped gingerly over two unconscious men, and then stood gazing at Minnie's lovely face for a moment before he reached down and gently took hold of both her hands. He pulled her up into a sitting position, and she mumbled something in her sleep as he cradled her head on his shoulder. Then he slipped his other arm beneath her knees and lifted her up against his chest. Fortunately she did not weigh very much, because his nerves were threatening to sap him of what strength he had left. He carried her back towards the door, scarcely able to believe he was going to make a clean getaway.

In his anxious state David forgot about the loose floorboard. With Minnie's extra weight in his arms the creak sounded as loud to him as the fatal report of a gunshot. Two men stirred, and then a third man opened his eyes and stared right at them. The RV was some way off, and David knew he had no chance of outrunning anyone while carrying Minnie in his arms. The man stared at them for a few seconds, but then simply closed his eyes again as his drunken stupor kept his brain from registering what he saw.

Out on the veranda David sat Minnie down on the swing, and gently tapped one of her cheeks. He needed her awake so she could walk back with him to the RV. Her eyes opened, and she stared up at him sleepily.

'Hi,' he whispered. 'How are you?'

She smiled, but then suddenly grimaced as she became aware of her body. 'I'm sore,' she replied, looking confused. 'Where am I? My head hurts...'

'You're at Gangbang Ranch,' David whispered.

'Christ,' she groaned, 'I drank too much.'

'That's not all you had too much of. Now come on, we've got to get out of here before they wake up.' He helped her to her feet, and quickly led her off the porch in the direction of the RV. He was relieved to see it exactly where he had left it. He then helped the naked girl – who had followed obediently behind him, only occasionally complaining about burrs and brambles – into the passenger's seat before taking his own place behind the wheel. He edged the vehicle slowly out onto the dirt track without using the headlights; there was just enough moonlight to make this possible. After that, he felt it was safe to make their way back towards the main road with the high beams on.

Minnie was not so sleepy that she did not realise they were driving back in the direction of the diner, and San Francisco was the other way. When she saw the roadhouse's neon sign, the place where it had all started, her stomach clenched, and she could scarcely believe it when they turned off the road towards it.

'Isn't this dangerous?' she asked breathlessly. 'If the bikers wake up and find out I'm gone, they might come looking for me.'

'It'll take them a while to realise you're gone,' David answered placidly. 'Besides, they have no way of knowing where you are, and this is probably the last place they'd look.' He drove the RV past the dimly lit diner to a remote corner of the large parking lot. Then he cut the engine and ordered her to get out.

Minnie studied his face for a moment, desperately trying to read his expression. She could not believe he was going to make her do anything else. She knew he had said she was to be another man's slave for *two* nights, and she had only been with the bikers for a few hours, but still…

'Get out,' he repeated quietly.

The thought crossed her mind that he was dumping her, but if that had been his intention, he would not have bothered to rescue her from the bikers while they were sleeping. Somewhat reassured by this thought, she finally obeyed him and stepped out onto the tarmac. It was very cold outside and her nipples immediately became hard, and she wrapped her arms around herself as she began shivering uncontrollably.

David remained seated behind the wheel, thinking. He wanted her to be totally compliant to his will, but he also needed her to consent to everything that happened to her, so she would be forced to recognise the fact that she had cooperated fully in her own humiliation and subjugation. And as he thought, he left her standing outside in the cold trying to cover herself with her arms and her hands whenever a trucker walked out of the diner. Every now and then a man would emerge, invariably lighting a cigarette, and pull up his collar before crunching his way across the parking lot, unaware of the fact that less then fifty yards away a girl stood naked and shivering, awaiting her master's instructions. But then, eventually, one of the drivers walking back towards his truck caught sight of her.

He was a huge bear of a man, but he was tall enough to carry the extra pounds well, so that they almost appeared to be muscle rather than fat. He had seen the RV pull in and recognised it from earlier. He had been on the road for over thirty years and had seen his fair share of strange sights and been involved in more than one unusual experience. He'd had his share of hitchhikers, too, some stunningly beautiful girls using their bodies to get where they wanted to go for free… and some not so beautiful, but equally enjoyable. After all, one warm pussy was much like any other in the dark.

The light came on in the RV, illuminating David where he sat behind the wheel and sending the trucker's thoughts into high gear. When he first saw the pair he had thought they were father and daughter, but then he heard the story that she was just hitching a ride with the Englishman. A girl turning up naked in the early hours of the morning was

85

not a unique occurrence; he had seen it happen a few times before – most truckers had. But he watched with growing interest as the Englishman emerged from the RV.

David lit a cigarette while enjoying the sight of Minnie's naked body trembling in the moonlight. 'Did you enjoy your experience tonight?' he asked her.

She nodded, relieved he had finally joined her and hoping he would let her get dressed soon. 'It was good, although kind of scary, too.'

'You did them all,' David said approvingly. 'I was watching you the whole time, just as I promised, and I counted. They all had you.'

'It was one hell of a train,' she agreed. The way he praised her made her feel proud, as though she had achieved something worthwhile. 'I thought it was never going to stop, and I just kept coming and coming.'

'You passed out in Angel's arms,' he mused. 'That was a lovely sight.'

'Did I please you?' she asked fervently. 'Did I make you happy, master?'

'You pleased me very much, and you made me very happy,' he assured her. 'You're doing very well, Minnie. You obey most instructions without hesitating, and you're learning how to please men.'

'Is that so?'

The gruff voice made them both start.

The trucker had moved closer and been listening to snatches of their conversation, and working out their relationship before making his move. 'So, she went round them all,' he said, eyeing Minnie up and down. 'That's some hard fucking for such a young thing to be doing. I guess you've trained her well.'

'She's one of the best slaves I've ever had,' David stated.

86

The bearded man looked Minnie up and down again, more slowly this time. 'Small tits,' he observed. 'May I?'

David saw no reason not to prolong the evening's entertainment. 'Be my guest,' he said.

The big man put his hands over her breasts and squeezed them. He grunted his approval of how firm they were, and moved them back and forth beneath his rough palms, pressing them cruelly into her chest. Then he pinched her hard nipples. She winced at his rough handling, and let out a little cry of protest when he shoved her back against the RV. He stepped to one side of her, thrust one hand between her thighs, and slipped two fingers along her smooth labia.

'You did that?' he asked, referring to her shaved pussy.

David eyed him carefully before nodding.

'Nice touch; goes real nice with these cute little tits of hers.' He thrust the same two fingers up into her warm, slick pussy, and finger-fucked her while staring up at the sky in concentration.

Minnie had no choice but to submit to his rude examination, and she even opened her legs a little to accommodate his large hand more comfortably. Her own eyes were fixed on David's face. Outwardly he appeared calm, but he was pulling hard on his cigarette as he watched another man's hand penetrating her. This scene did not have as many players as the grand opening act, but she sensed that his proximity to the action was exciting him. She wondered just how much more her master would force her to suffer before the night was over, and it would have disturbed her to know that David was wondering if he had gone too far already. She needed to believe he knew exactly what he was doing, that he was always in control of himself and would never tell her to endure more than he knew she could bear.

Meanwhile, the trucker, unaware of and untroubled by the thoughts of the principle players, pulled Minnie away from the RV and forced her down to her knees before him. 'Is she in training?' he asked David while nonchalantly unzipping his jeans.

'Yes, she is,' David told him frankly.

'Thought so.' The man pushed her head back, pulled his cock out of his pants, and fed it carefully between her lips into her warm wet mouth.

Closing her eyes she sucked him instinctively, but it was her master she was striving to please as she did so, the eagerness of her tongue expressing her happiness that he was there with her.

'She all yours?' the man continued questioning David as he rested his hands lightly on Minnie's head, prepared to take control of it but first waiting to see just how good a job she did of sucking his dick before he did.

'Let's just say she's my ward,' David replied, intrigued by the trucker's knowledge of the slave and master relationship, and by his offhand, almost dismissive, attitude towards it. 'She's mine until it's time to release her into the care of someone who truly needs her.'

The man let out a soft groan, and pulled his rigid penis out of Minnie's mouth. 'Gotta hand it to you, baby,' he said, 'you're a damn good cocksucker. You must have been head of your class.' He winked at David. 'Now up against the van, baby, palms up, legs spread. You know the drill.'

Minnie quickly assumed the position. This man made her nervous. It disturbed her the way he could carry on a conversation while she blew him; the way he could ignore her fervently sucking mouth as if she wasn't making him feel anything at all. His cold, almost mechanical attitude had her thoughts and feelings in turmoil as she tried to make sense of it. Her submissiveness stemmed in great part from her need for attention, and from the mysterious power it gave her to suck the sexual marrow from her master, both physically and spiritually, by giving him absolute power over her, in every sense. This man had no marrow to speak of, and it frightened her.

She moaned as she felt his cock bully its way up into her pussy again, this time from behind. How big he was presented a logistical problem to her tight vagina, but he obviously did not care. He just kept pushing his erection into her as she cried out softly in mingled pain and pleasure, and David watched silently.

At last he had packed his rod all the way up inside her, at which point he grabbed hold of her waist and began moving slowly in and out of her, forcing her to take his entire penis every time.

'How long she been with you?' the man asked David as he fucked her casually.

'A few days.'

'That all? You must be good. She's very compliant.'

'Totally.'

Minnie found herself frustrated when the trucker did not pick up the pace, and she pushed back against him to see if it would inspire him. He responded by spanking her with such force that the smacking sound resounded across the parking lot.

She gasped in shock and pain, but managed to hold back an outraged cry by biting her lip and glancing over at David's impassive face. He seemed to be deliberately avoiding her eyes, so there was no way for her to know if the scene was still pleasing him.

'Why'd you bring her back here?' the man resumed his unhurried interrogation while he continued fucking her in much the same way.

David shrugged; he did not feel obliged to share the workings of his mind with a complete stranger.

The trucker slipped out of Minnie abruptly. 'Turn around,' he snapped. 'Is it nice and warm inside your van?'

'Yes, I left the heat on,' David replied.

'The poor girl looks cold, but I know a better way to get her blood flowing.'

'Oh?' David sensed an interesting development. 'What did you have in mind?'

He pointed across the parking lot at a large meatpacking wagon. 'That's what Norwegians do when they're freezing their butts off, roll around in the snow. Ain't got no snow, but I do got the next best thing.'

David smiled at the suggestion, so the man promptly grabbed Minnie by the arm, and pulled her across the parking lot to the meatpacking truck while David followed.

'Please,' she whimpered, 'I'm already so cold!' It did not surprise her that her protest was completely ignored.

Her captor pulled open the bar locking the metal doors closed, and the clank of steel against steel was followed by a hissing white cloud of freezing cold air rushing out of the trailer. It engulfed the young woman, who moaned pitifully.

'Get in,' the driver commanded, and when she did not obey him at once he thrust his hand between her thighs, and heaved her up into the trailer. Then he climbed in after her, and as soon as David had followed them in, he leaned out and pulled the doors closed behind them.

For a moment they all stood in total darkness, and then the cab was illuminated by a dull red glow as the trucker switched on the lights. Then he began looking around for some flexi clips while Minnie and David studied the sides of beef hanging from hooks in the ceiling. She could imagine how the carcasses felt as she shivered violently and hugged herself, desperately wishing David would look at her.

'Guess you like suspending them, too?' The man had found a number of ropes, and he handed some to David. Then he stepped behind Minnie, yanked her arms up over her head, and snapped the flexi clips around her wrists.

Her pleading expression had no effect on David whatsoever as he bent over to secure her ankles.

'Don't worry about her mouth,' the driver said, 'this wagon's soundproof.' He grabbed Minnie by the waist and hoisted her up. A hook caught the flexi grips around her wrists, and when he let go of her she was left suspended from it just like a freshly skinned carcass. Only she was still very much alive, and her fear was expressed by the faint white clouds of her shallow, panting breaths.

'Please, David,' she begged, 'I've done everything you said. Please, I'm so cold…' Her body was stretched taut. Her ribs showed through her fine skin, and her belly was a sunken valley beneath the snowy mounds of her breasts and above her shaved mound, which shone like polished marble in the frosty air.

Her plea fell on deaf ears, however, as the two men removed their belts, at which point she whimpered in terror. She knew the intense cold would make every stroke of the leather across her strained flesh ten times more painful. The icy temperatures also intensified the painful heat in her shoulder blades caused by hanging suspended from her wrists. She knew each and every stroke of the leather would hurt like nothing else ever had. They would feel like being cut by a knife over and over again, and she was terrified.

'Oh, please don't do this,' she begged as the men took up their positions, and her scream as the first blows fell threatened to shatter every inch of ice off the sides of the truck, and she kept on screaming as they took turns whipping her firm back and quivering buttocks.

'Scream all you like, baby,' the trucker taunted her, clearly deriving much more pleasure from beating her than he had from merely fucking her. David found his enthusiasm contagious, and he laid into the poor girl's bottom with a vengeance he had never displayed before. The other man's cruel laughter, and her desperate cries of pain, lifted him to a heightened, almost trancelike, state. Even after her head fell forward and she stopped begging for mercy, he kept on flogging her relentlessly. He was no longer bothering to wait his turn; both men were hitting her at the same time, wherever the mood struck them, and more than once their belts intersected to forge a burning red cross in her white skin.

At last, strangely exhausted by his efforts, David paused between strokes, and abruptly realised Minnie was as limp and motionless as the skinned carcasses hanging around her. 'Stop!' he yelled.

The trucker's arm froze in mid-flight, and David saw the mad gleam in his eyes. He was a man who would give Minnie exactly what she wanted. She would become the centre of his universe. Unfortunately, it would probably kill her.

'That's enough,' David said quietly but firmly.

The man lowered the belt. 'That was fucking great,' he gasped. 'I've never beaten a girl that hard. Hey, baby, did you enjoy that?'

There was no response from Minnie, whose flesh bore a sinister resemblance to the garish neon sign outside. It was tinged with blue, while the back of her body was striped with red welts.

'Fucking hell,' the trucker whispered in terrified awe, 'I

think we—'

'No, we didn't,' David cut him off before he could say the unthinkable. He was angry with himself for losing control and joining in this man's cruel and mindless frenzy. He quickly reached up and undid the clips around her wrist. 'Grab hold of her,' he ordered, 'and help me get her back to the RV.'

The man did as he was told, and between them they carried the limp and silent girl back to the camper, and laid her gently across the couch.

'What you gonna do now, man?' the trucker asked David in a hushed voice, still obviously believing they had gone too far.

David, however, knew Minnie was perfectly all right. Her breathing had slowed because of the cold temperatures, and the multiple orgasms she had suffered while they beat her had completely exhausted her mind and body, which were already worn out by drinking too much earlier, not to mention being gangbanged. He knew some warm towels and a few shots of vodka would set her right in no time.

'What you gonna do?' the anxious man repeated, staring down at Minnie's peacefully smiling face.

'I'll take care of it,' David told him sombrely, enjoying his discomfort. 'No need for the two of us to get dragged in on this thing.'

The driver quickly started backing away towards the door. 'You're right,' he agreed, and turned on his heels.

Less than a minute later there was the sound of an engine starting up, followed by the roar as a truck sped out of the parking lot.

David smiled to himself, and quickly began attending to Minnie.

First he turned her gently over onto her stomach, and

then he pulled some ice from the freezer and wrapped it up in a towel to rest it across her striped bottom. That would take the sting out of her welts and reduce any swelling. He would worry about the marks on her back later. Right now the important thing was to cover her with several layers of blankets, and supplement their warmth with a couple of hot water bottles tucked in between her body and the back of the sofa. Finally, he turned up the battery heater.

She was still very cold, but as he sat down beside her he could detect some warmth returning to her body and he knew it would not be long before she came round. He caressed her hair, and tucked it behind one of her ears the way she always did, thinking about what a completely different girl she was now than when he met her in Seattle only a few days before. She had been a street waif then, unsure of herself and of her sexuality, unaware of everything she was capable of.

She moaned, and turned her face towards him. There was still the trace of smile on her lips, and David responded to the sight with a smile of his own. She was asleep and safe, and everything was all right with the world. He felt like getting some sleep himself, but first it would be wiser to get as far away from Gangbang Ranch as possible. The bikers probably would not bother to come looking for her, but it was best not to take any chances. He imagined they would spend the next few months shooting pool and drinking beer and talking about the night that girl came in with the Englishman who looked old enough to be her father, and about how they gangbanged her until she passed out.

David stood up, and lifted the sheets covering her to have a final look at her body. Her bottom and her back were marked from the beating she had suffered in the meatpacking truck. He would have to buy some ointment and massage it soothingly into her skin later. But for now the most important thing was for her to sleep and recover the energy her body needed.

He slipped into the driver's seat, turned the radio on at a volume that would help keep him awake but not disturb Minnie, drove out of the parking lot, and headed south. The highway was deserted; it was just him and the sleeping girl and Van Morrison *on a lovely night for a dance under the stars*.

Chapter Five

Minnie slept straight through the next day.

When it was late enough for the stores to be open, David pulled into a sparsely populated town with no name – at least he could not find it on the map – and bought himself a laptop computer after telephoning his friend, Justin, in England to find out his e-mail address. The time for their rendezvous in Miami was approaching.

He also bought a few other supplies at a supermarket, and when he returned to the RV with his purchases, Minnie was still asleep. He left her that way and continued driving south. It was a glorious morning, and he resisted his need for sleep until he came across a lonely cove with just enough room for one vehicle. He'd had enough company for a while and was craving solitude, and found it between two large rocks hidden from the road at the edge of a line of trees.

He parked, and then pulled two chairs outside along with his folding table. While Minnie continued sleeping, he laid some food out and then uncorked a bottle of Chablis. He poured himself a glass and sliced into the Brie he had bought earlier. Happy with his light lunch, he settled comfortably in his chair facing the sun and opened up the manual for his new laptop. Within seconds, he was asleep.

The caress of a cool breeze, and the sound of water lapping softly on the shore, woke him. The sun had set. It was the mystical touch of moonlight on his eyelids that penetrated his dreams and helped the elements rouse him. Then he became aware of a soft red flickering light, and turned his head to discover that Minnie was awake, and had started a fire. They had learned early in their partnership that they both enjoyed the natural warmth of burning wood, and he saw her striding along the beach carrying several branches the sea had washed up.

'You're awake,' she observed soberly.

'Yes…' He yawned and stretched, a little stiff from sleeping in a chair but feeling refreshed nonetheless. 'Thanks for not waking me.'

She dropped the branches beside the fire, and began feeding them one by one into the crackling flames. 'I could say the same to you,' she pointed out, an odd tone in her voice. She was wearing one of his button-down shirts with the sleeves rolled up, and it was so big on her that the front tails hung down almost to her knees. Her hair was down and several strands were wafting up in the chilly breeze. She looked as young and beautiful as ever, but her large eyes seemed darker, with a hint of a very adult sadness in them.

David studied the fire, and then the additional food she had laid out on the table beside him. 'You've been busy,' he said. 'Good girl.'

'Supper,' she said listlessly.

'How did you know?' he asked ambiguously.

'You told me that when it felt right, I would know,' she answered, and sat down opposite him. She looked down at the food as if thinking about eating, but she did not touch it. 'It's funny,' she went on quietly, 'I *know* I had a reason for running away from home, but deep down I think I was also looking for something… something I could only find by getting as far away from my life as possible.'

David poured himself another glass of the Chablis he

had enjoyed earlier, laid a smoked oyster on top of a cracker, and popped them both in his mouth. 'Mm,' he said as he chewed. 'Travel does broaden the mind. The trouble is, some people go around the world and see less than a mole wearing a blindfold, whereas others can see the whole universe from a wheelchair in a basement.'

'That's what you were talking about the night you took me into the woods and tied me between those two trees, wasn't it?' she asked seriously. 'That's what you meant when you were talking about the brain being different from the mind, and how different minds work differently.'

'You could have found yourself on that little farm you grew up on, Minnie.' He poured her some wine. 'You just didn't know where to look.'

She took a quick sip, not really tasting it as she pursued her thoughts. 'I would have missed out on a lot of fun,' she concluded.

'On a lot of pleasure,' David corrected her. 'Fun was being buck naked on the beach with your mother when you were a little girl. Pleasure is being fucked naked on the beach by four young bucks.'

She laughed at his play on words. 'It's another mind thing, isn't it?'

He nodded, intent on finishing the Brie he had started on earlier.

'What's that quote about "when I was a child"?' she asked him.

'It's from *Corinthians*,' he replied, after washing down the cheese with another mouthful of wine. '"When I was a child, I spoke as a child, I understood as a child, I thought as a child, but when I became a man, I put away childish things".'

'*That's* the one. I never really understood it before, but I

98

do now. It's about knowing, isn't it? I ran laughing down the beach with my mother, but I didn't know why. Yet now that I'm older, I can walk along the same stretch of sand and take so much more from it. I can take pleasure, not just a fleeting moment's pleasure, but a real, deep pleasure that in some way helps define me.'

David concealed how impressed he was by her insight because he did not want his praise to distract her from her thoughts, which he was very interested in hearing.

'You're old,' she stated abruptly.

'Thanks for the compliment.' He laughed to cover up the fact that she had succeeded in hurting his feelings, at least for an instant.

'Oh, not in that way,' she said dismissively. 'I mean in your mind. You knew I could find myself without travelling the world, didn't you?'

'Well, sort of,' he said, his pride somewhat assuaged. 'But travel is a wonderful thing, too.' He looked out across the ocean, enjoying the breeze caressing his face and his hair. 'You just have to collect the right postcards.'

She gave him a puzzled look, cocking her head in that adorable way of hers.

'There are people who travel a thousand miles to see a place,' he went on, 'and then spend the rest of their time in shops buying postcards to prove they've been there, and yet they weren't, not really. They travelled thousands of miles just to go shopping just like they do at home. The leaning tower of Pisa could fall down right behind them and they wouldn't even know it until they saw it on the evening news.'

Minnie's head was still cocked to one side, her eyes as wide as the proverbial puppy's as she struggled to understand him.

'Sorry.' He smiled ruefully. 'Like you said, I'm old – an old cynic who thinks he knows it all.'

'That doesn't make you wrong,' she pointed out sagely.

David decided that after spending the last couple of nights watching her being fucked and punished by other men it was time to enjoy her again himself. He would kiss and suckle her breasts until she moaned. He would caress her nubile legs and her smooth, warm pussy, and then he would slide his erection into her and fuck her harder than he ever had. And then he would come so deep inside her she would never be able to forget him.

The sun was just rising above the horizon when they awoke, lying together on the beach. Some seagulls taking advantage of the early light were already fishing and arguing over their catch.

David leaned over Minnie and planted a kiss on her forehead to wish her a silent good morning. He sat up, rested his elbows on his knees, and gazed down at her. He would miss looking at her like this. With her face relaxed in sleep, she looked even younger than her nineteen years. He could not resist taking a peek between her legs, and he saw that her pussy lips showed just how much she had been used lately, including by himself only a few hours before. Her labia was fuller than usual, and had been beaten and stroked to a lovely rose colour. She looked absolutely delicious; he had to resist the urge to sink his teeth into her.

She opened her eyes, and caught him staring down at her.

'Big day,' he said.

'Big day,' she echoed, sitting up.

They sat watching the ocean for a while in silence. It was low tide and the water was calm. There were two boats visible on the horizon, gliding in opposite directions, and David did not fail to notice the symbolism.

'Feel like a morning swim?' he asked her.

'Sure,' she said, 'why not?'

'Why not, indeed.'

They walked over to the water hand-in-hand and waded in up to their waists before diving headfirst into the gentle waves. The water was refreshingly cool, not shockingly cold, and they swam in opposite directions for a while. David was enjoying the exercise, and the lovely feeling of having a beach all to himself.

It was Minnie who started heading towards shore first. He followed her, and took hold of her on the firm sand where the water licked around their ankles. He made love to her there, with the edges of the waves caressing them in rhythm with their own undulating motions. Then, afterwards, they moved up the beach onto their towel and lay side-by-side on their backs soaking up the morning sun's relaxing heat.

'I won't ever forget you,' she said after a while, 'or this moment. I'll always think about you.'

They turned their heads to look at each other. Their eyes met, and they smiled.

'I'll never forget you either, Minnie,' he said truthfully. Yet how often he would actually think about her was another story.

At the bus station in Fort Bragg a handful of travellers were waiting for their ride, some of them sitting beside veritable mountains of luggage.

Minnie returned to the platform from using the phone inside the small building where she had purchased her ticket home. She was wearing a new pair of tight jeans and a short-sleeved shirt that ended just below her breasts in the latest fashion. Her hair was down, as usual, and she looked radiantly beautiful. They had stopped at a shopping centre along the way to buy her some badly needed clothes.

'How is she?' David asked her, referring to Minnie's mother, whom she had just called to inform her that her daughter was safe and sound, and coming home.

'Overjoyed,' Minnie said, feeling relieved. 'She said she was afraid I was never coming back.'

'What did you tell her?'

'I told her I'd seen all I wanted to see, and that now it was time to come home and start doing something with my life. When she asked me why I ran away, I told her we'd talk about that when I got back.'

David handed her the small bag containing her scant possessions. Her bus was pulling up, and he walked her over to it. 'It's a shame you never made it to San Francisco,' he heard himself say, and realised he was reluctant to let her go now the time had come.

'I don't need those postcards any more,' she replied, and then reached up and planted a soft kiss on his lips while tucking her hair neatly behind her ear. 'And every time I travel, it'll be for real, just like you said.' She turned, and started up the steps into the bus. 'I might even go back to school,' she called back to him over her shoulder, 'and study medicine.'

David smiled, and waited for the bus to pull out of the station before he turned down Main Street in search of a beer. He had enjoyed Minnie very much, although not quite as much as his Lapp sisters, but he was happy to be on his own again. After spending so much time by himself he had learned to enjoy his own company more than anything, or anyone, else.

The establishment David ended up in was a bit warm and stuffy, and set too close to a busy intersection, but it looked like the only place in town so he pulled up a stool at the bar. The half dozen or so men in the place were all staring intently into their drinks, and one old timer who was missing a hand was concentrating on chasing shots of whisky with German beer.

The bartender scraped the head off a beer with a wooden paddle, which he dropped into a jug of water. 'Fine day,' he said, setting the mug in front of David.

'It's a fine day, indeed,' David replied, sensing the bartender was desperate for some intelligent conversation, and obliging him with an opening.

The man's face lit up. 'That's an English accent, isn't it?'

'You guessed it.'

'Been to London once myself. Loved the people, but the city was dirty as hell. There was trash everywhere.'

'That's London.' David helped himself to a peanut from the dish the bartender had brought him along with his drink.

'But I loved all the old buildings and the history,' the man went on eagerly. 'We've got our own history right here, too, you know. There was a big Indian battle here about a hundred-and-fifty years ago. Wild place in them days.' He seemed to be trying to unload a lifetime's worth of conversations on one customer, and hardly stopped to catch his breath. 'You could get a room, a shave and a woman for the night for just two bits, all under this roof. Of course, that's all changed now, although you can still get your hair cut here. Not many bars in this country do that for you any more.'

'Sure would like to see that,' David said, now eager to escape the verbal tirade he had unleashed. He got up, looked around, and spotted a curtain made of colourful beads separating the bar from another room beyond. 'Is that it?' he asked hopefully. 'Can I get a haircut in there? I could use a bit of a trim.'

'That's the place.'

David walked towards the curtain, taking his beer with him.

'Best barber in Fort Bragg, old Tom is,' the bartender called after him. 'Like one of them Indians from back yonder with those scissors, though, so better watch your neck.' He laughed.

The beads swept together like the rushes along a windy creek as David stepped into the backroom.

Old Tom was obviously related to the bartender, possibly even his twin brother they looked so much alike. Tom, however, was wonderfully quiet and reserved. David exchanged a glance with him that communicated everything that was necessary, and headed for the vacant seat Tom indicated with a slight nod of his head.

The coffee table in the small waiting area was strewn with the usual magazines, and David selected a computer monthly, hoping it might help him understand all the things he could do with his new laptop. He sat in the chair, began flipping through it, and came to an article on newsgroups.

He had spent much of the last few years in the wilderness and, consequently, his knowledge of software and hardware was as extensive as his knowledge of flora in the region of the Upper Volta; he was years behind the times. Given his recent purchase of a state-of-the-art portable computer, and his desire to come to grips with it, his interest in the subject was keen. He had a basic knowledge of the World Wide Web, and he had done a bit of surfing on the Internet. He had used e-mail and he certainly was not a technophobe, but newsgroups were a novel development for him, and he read the article with interest.

He learned that newsgroups had come into existence for the purpose of bringing likeminded individuals together around a common subject. Only four paragraphs into the article, he had decided to set up a newsgroup of his own dedicated to sadomasochism, and then he discovered that whatever group he could possibly conceive of already existed. They were all there. The article even went so far as to list a few of the more bizarre sites, the majority of which were dedicated to sex. In fact, almost all the sites beginning with an *alt* prefix were of an adult nature.

He was intrigued, and excited. This was as good a way as any to learn about technology, while having fun with people who thought and felt much as he did about male domination and female submission.

David left the barbershop with shorter hair, a keen interest in newsgroups, and the computer magazine tucked inside his jacket.

Later that same day, David drove a bit further south but decided to stop before he got to San Francisco. He found a small campsite with all the necessary facilities, and decided to stay there for the night. He restocked his fridge with beers at the small camp shop, made some dinner, and then settled down to an evening in front of the computer.

The machine was already set up for Internet access with a wireless modem, and the first thing he did was send a message to Justin back in England concerning the sale of his house, and asking him when he planned on arriving in Miami.

With that taken care of, he loaded up some of the newsgroups listed in the magazine he had taken from the barbershop, and promptly began subscribing to a few. He soon learned that the groups with binaries in their title contained images.

He downloaded a few pictures, and realised that much of what was out their on the Web had been hijacked by commercial companies trying to persuade members to visit their sites. It was not long, however, before he learned what size files were the most productive, and avoided the header messages usually employed by the more commercial sites. He looked at the section under the *sender* column as well, and searched out personal names, which normally meant the sender was a genuine group member and not a company trying to sidetrack him.

His laptop seemed to warp time, because when he glanced at his watch he discovered with a shock that he had been downloading images for almost three hours, and during that time he had seen beautiful women in some of the most depraved poses he could ever have imagined.

He had drunk a few beers while he surfed the Net, and he enjoyed stroking his cock close to orgasm, but now he stopped and got up to use the bathroom. Then he pulled another beer out of the fridge intending to continue relaxing with both his newest toy and his oldest. He had already learned how to open up new folders, and he filed away some of his favourite photographs in them. As a doctor, especially one with his particular interests, he was always eager to learn more about the human mind and how it attempts to bring order where there was once only chaos. He stripped naked, and spent about fifteen minutes categorising his folders before he realised what he was doing.

The deep silence inside the van focused all his attention on his luminous screen's mysterious portal into a virtual dimension. He felt as though he could lean forward and push his head beyond the flat screen as though it was the surface of a luminous pool. Then he would be able to see into this surreal and flowing world where beautiful women fucked their bosses the moment they arrived at the office; where pizza delivery boys ejaculated over sliced pepperoni for grateful customers who answered the door in garter belts and stockings and six-inch stiletto heels; where no woman ever said 'no' and every man had a cock worthy of a prize stallion.

'Jesus Christ,' he said out loud, 'what am I doing? I'm making separate folders for women with big breasts, small breasts, for redheads, brunettes, and blondes. I have folders for shaved cunts, hairy cunts, tattooed arses, dildo cams. Am I going fucking nuts?'

He pushed the laptop away from him, and picked up his beer.

When his heartbeat had slowed to normal, David pulled the computer back towards him and composed another e-mail to Justin, asking him again how the sale of his house was going. For a moment he considered shutting off the computer and going to bed, but his curiosity was still up, and the portal into cyberspace remained open as he continued his virtual journey.

To prevent visual overload he searched the groups for text messages, and signed up for one dedicated to swingers in the San Francisco area. He downloaded a few hundred headers, and trawled for those that looked the most interesting. He ended up downloading hundreds of headers and was amazed at how some of the messages contained actual addresses to people's homes as well as phone numbers.

He did not want to admit it, but he was feeling a bit lonely without Minnie, so he consoled himself with the candy box of delights that was the San Francisco swingers. He read up on how to answer messages. It was a mean old world out there. There were warnings about giving out your addresses and telephone numbers too soon, and it was supposedly not a good idea to part with money for a promised night of sex. But all these snippets of cynical advice were belied at the bottom of the page where it said, *The vast majority of newsgroup subscribers are genuine and, while you may come across some people with their own motives for joining the group, by remembering the few guidelines above, you should be able to encounter likeminded people and make many new friends. Newsgroups are an excellent, quick and efficient way to meet other people.*

David checked out a few more newsgroups and downloaded a lot more messages. There appeared to be some pretty decent women out there itching for sex, either that or they had a fetish for being photographed naked on coffee tables whilst polishing various household ornaments between their stocking-clad thighs. Whatever the case, David had a lot of fun with his new laptop, and he thought he would reply to a few of these women and see if he could score some action for the couple of days he intended to stay in the city. He read the instructions again carefully and remembered to post the reply to the sender and not the group, otherwise the whole world, figuratively speaking, could read what he had to say.

It was another hour before he finally managed to pull himself away from the screen and turn off the computer. Then he went to bed and slipped into the more natural virtual world of dreams.

David's breakfast was more eye-candy. He switched on his laptop the moment he got up, and was surprised at how excited he was that his e-mail inbox was flashing an envelope icon that read *You have mail*.

He had seven messages, and the first one he opened was a note from Justin in England. Being around the same age as each other, both men tended to treat e-mails as if they were old-fashioned telegrams where you had to pay by the word, and Justin was a lot worse than David in this respect. His message read, *Sold Camelot. Coming across in a week or so. Contact you soon*. And that was all.

David clicked on the next message, and discovered it was from a woman who wanted to meet him later that day, but only if he could send her proof, in the form of a photograph, that his erect penis was at least nine inches long and as thick as her wrist. She neglected to tell him just how thick her wrist was, however, and without the benefit of a scanner or the necessary software, David was proving nothing.

Within the first twenty minutes he was online, however, Cindy – it was amazing how many women were named Cindy – sent him an additional five messages, each more demanding than the last. She even attached some pictures of herself. She was definitely an attractive woman, but her demanding attitude did not appeal to David in the least. For one insane moment he considered making a date with her just to teach her a lesson, but he controlled himself and ignored her e-mails. It was a personal vow of his that he would only train and chastise women who wanted it. Cindy knew what she wanted, and he hoped she got it, but she was not going to get it from him. The last he heard from her was a message in which she called him all sorts of insulting names. Attractive she was, eloquent she was not.

Most of the other messages he received were no more promising. There were a few from bored housewives looking to mess around with someone in the afternoons before their husbands got home from work, and there were some David sensed had actually been written by husbands for their wives. These were more interesting to him because of the power and control aspects they revealed concerning the relationship of the senders, and he kept them for later consideration.

With only a few days to spend in the city, he was not looking for anything too heavy. Nevertheless, he was about to get it in the form of a message with the header, *Frisco Filly Needs Breaking*.

That was another lesson David had learned pretty early on – if you wanted someone to read your e-mail, it was best to sound bright and cheerful and interesting. *Frisco Filly Needs Breaking* was an attention catching subject line that did its job.

He promptly read the accompanying message.

Frisco filly seeks cowboy for riding and general saddle work. Ranch owners welcome. Into rope work, buckles and boots.

Cute. David thought the woman definitely sounded like fun, and then he noticed the attachment. He quickly clicked on it, and the image opened up. To his delight she looked as much fun as she sounded.

She appeared to be in her late twenties, or a well-preserved thirty-something, and her shoulder-length blonde hair was topped with a white Stetson hat. She was topless above a tight pair of jeans unzipped to reveal girlish white panties. She was posing out in the desert, a white Caddy with bullhorns on the hood and red leather trim parked behind her. She was all gleaming white teeth and gorgeous

110

breasts.

But more than all that – and David could scarcely believe it – he actually recognised her.

He was looking at a picture of Donna from San Diego. Or rather, Donna from Frisco, as she now called herself. But whatever part of the west coast she preferred, David would always remember her as Donna from the *International Club* in Karachi!

He slumped down in his chair and reached for the cereal box, never once taking his eyes off the screen, not even as he ate his breakfast. Finally, he pushed the bowl away and said out loud, 'I thought you would never escape from Khan.' He smiled, and was surprised at how happy he was to see her face again after so many years. He would have to meet with her, but now he was faced with a dilemma.

The last time he had seen Donna she was being fucked senseless over the railing of Khan's yacht off Karachi while someone filmed the action. The time before that, David had possessed her himself, several times, in the *International Club*. He had tied her down and caned her until she begged him to fuck her. Then he had left her behind even after she pleaded with him to help her get away.

He made some tea and sipped it as he looked at the gorgeous woman staring back at him from the screen. His guilt at leaving her had been tremendous, and it came back to haunt him now. He consoled himself with the knowledge that he had still been learning how to survive himself back when he knew her, and had been in no position to help her.

He remembered only too well that the last person who attempted to rescue her, a Japanese businessman, had taken an undesired starring role in the film on Khan's boat, after which he was never seen again.

David had not wanted to suffer the same fate, hence he

ignored Donna's plea to help her escape. He was not a coward, he told himself firmly. He was a survivor.

By the time he finished his tea, all the memories of his time in Pakistan and Afghanistan had flooded back and he was forced to deal with them. There was not one good reason why Donna would ever want to see him again, a man who had fucked her, and then abandoned her. Nonetheless, David managed to convince himself that if she was a Frisco swinger, then she had recovered from her experiences in the *International Club* and, amazingly enough, remained psychologically unscarred, or at least unperturbed, by the memory of the sexual acts she had been forced into by her customers.

He studied her features closely, searching for any evidence of tension in her lovely face. She appeared perfectly relaxed and happy, and there was no hint of coercion in her sexy stance.

David considered himself selfish in the extreme, but for old time's sake he wanted to see her. He moved the cursor across to the *Reply to Sender* button, and clicked it. But before he began typing his message, he decided not to refer to their previous encounter until she agreed to meet him.

He fired off a response, and paced the RV in the hope that she was online at the moment and would get back to him straightaway.

Over an hour passed and he still had not received a reply, so he jumped into the driver's seat and drove a little further south. Then he stopped to make something to eat, and eagerly checked his mail.

He had no new messages.

Disappointed, he read the ones he had stored earlier and came to the conclusion that if Donna was off-line he might as well make use of some of the other women who had written to him. He answered every message, and within minutes he received a reply. It was from a man called Oscar, and he was desperate to see his wife, Tammy, fucked by a stranger with a large cock. It almost sounded like a plea for help, and the tone of the mail told David more about the man than it did about his wife.

The message revealed that Oscar was considerably older than Tammy, and that he adored her but was not able to give her the satisfaction she needed between the sheets. Oscar felt he did not deserve to be married to such a beautiful young woman, and that his prick did not measure up to the job of pleasing her. If he could just give Tammy what he knew she wanted, he was sure she would be happy with him, because that was all he wanted; to make her happy. He loved her, and went through her linen basket every night checking her panties for telltale signs of the lover he suspected she must have.

David recognised the type. The man was submissive, and he wanted to worship his wife for living with him. He replied to Oscar by asking, *Does Tammy want this?*

Within minutes he received an answer. *She says she's not sure.* The man had used an instant messaging service to get back to David, and they now proceeded to have an online conversation.

Describe her, David typed.

She's twenty-eight and has blonde, waist-length hair. She's slim with blue eyes and a beautiful smile.

Is she with you now?

Yes, she's right next to me. She's very nervous.

Have you asked her about any boyfriends? David pursued his enquiry.

She says there's no one, but I found some stains on her panties and I'm sure there's a guy where she works who's doing her.

How do you feel about that?

There was a long pause before the man responded. *I'm okay with it as long as Tammy stays with me. She knows she can have whatever she wants.*

This guy who works with Tammy, is he big?

Yes.

Do you think he makes Tammy do dirty things? Does she dress like his slut when she goes out for his cock? David was almost certain Oscar's wife was not screwing anyone, but he knew the man had fed his fantasy so many times it was the only meal he could eat.

She puts on high-heeled shoes and tight blouses for him just so he can rip them off her and bang her like the slut she is.

Are you okay with me fucking her? David typed.

There was another long pause before the reply arrived. *Yes. Maybe she'll see how much I love her and she'll stop cheating on me behind my back.*

I like sluts, David informed him. *I might want to treat her like one. Does she give good head?*

Yes.

Great. Tell her that when I arrive I expect her to do exactly as I say. I'm not used to being disobeyed. Does she understand? David upped the ante, but apparently he timed his moment perfectly.

She says she's scared but she'll try for my sake.

Good, and I expect the same obedience from you. Do you understand?

I'll do as you say, the man replied submissively.

Once I step through the door, your wife is mine and you're powerless to stop me no matter what I do to her. Are we agreed on this?

114

Agreed.

David asked for their address, received it, and had just switched off with Oscar when he finally received a reply from Donna.

Chapter Six

It was almost nine-thirty at night before David drove his RV into Rushmore Crescent, a quiet suburban street decorated with palm trees. Behind the arboreal markers stretched pleasant lawns and gardens leading up to large and expensive homes.

He was near the end of the road before the number he was looking for came into view. Although he was confident in himself, this was new territory for him, and he ran over in his mind several scenarios, including how to extricate himself if something went wrong or did not feel right. He pulled slowly up the drive listening to the crunch of gravel beneath the wheels. In this quiet neighbourhood it sounded to him like a fireworks display announcing his arrival, but no one looked out to investigate.

It took three rings of the doorbell before a middle-aged man finally answered. He was a bit shorter than David and his hair was thinning, but he had a pleasant face and he looked fit in his jeans and T-shirt.

'Oscar?' David asked.

The man nodded, and stretched out his hand. 'You must be David.'

David shook his hand but gave him only a faint smile, not wanting to appear overly friendly. He was, after all, there to fuck the man's wife and play a part in their sexual fantasies, a part which was not polite and considerate.

Oscar stepped aside, and gestured for David to pass.

It was a big house and tastefully decorated and furnished.

The living room was warm and inviting despite its overriding white decor. Several leather chairs were scattered across the plush carpet, and a contrastingly colourful rug was spread out across the hearth of a large stone fireplace. The fire was lit, and David appreciated the warmth it gave out; San Francisco could be very hot during the day and yet quite cold at night. The room's casual intimacy was further enhanced by candlelight provided by scented wax.

'Would you care for a drink?' Oscar asked him, rather formally.

'A beer would be nice,' David replied. He seated himself in one of the chairs beside the fire and waited patiently, but his drink was slow in coming. Subdued voices from the kitchen suggested Tammy was discussing the night's upcoming events with her husband, and suffering from cold feet. *Or from a cold pussy*, David thought, smiling to himself.

Eventually Oscar returned with a glass of beer he handed to his guest with an unsteady hand. 'You're English,' he remarked inanely, seating himself across from David on a couch.

'That's right, I'm English, and your wife's getting it from some guy at work,' David stated bluntly, skirting the small talk and going straight for the jugular.

Surprisingly enough, Oscar seemed to welcome his direct approach. 'He's a bastard,' he declared, opening up. 'He's always chatting Tammy up at company parties and touching her cheek and putting his arm around her waist.'

'And that makes you think he's fucking her behind your back?'

'I can see it,' Oscar answered ardently, leaning forward. 'The way he looks over her shoulder at me and smirks, it's

117

obvious. It's like he's saying, "Hey man, I'm drilling your wife and there's fuck all you can do about it".'

David put his drink on a shelf built into the fireplace. 'If it upsets you so much, why do you want me to drill her, too?'

'Because I can't get the vision of him banging her out of my head.' Oscar looked and sounded increasingly agitated. 'I see them at it in my mind all the time, rutting like animals. I even come home and check the sheets because I know the dirty bastard is doing her in my own bed. It's driving me fucking crazy.'

'Have you found anything to confirm your suspicions?' David asked reasonably. 'Any evidence at all?'

Oscar shook his head. 'She's too clever for that. A few times I've come home and there'll be clean sheets on the bed even though I know for a fact she'd only changed them a couple of days ago. So I figured if I let her have her fun with someone who isn't going to take her away, that she'll stay with me. I can give her anything she wants; I run my own business and it's doing better every day. I just want her to stay with me.'

'You're not being honest with me, Oscar,' David said quietly, and clearly hit a nerve.

His host sat back abruptly, and rubbed his forehead as if in an effort to straighten out his thoughts and determine just how much to tell this English stranger. It was then they both noticed Tammy had slipped silently into the room.

David turned his head her way and gave her a cold stare, expertly concealing the fact that he was struck by her beauty. Oscar had every right to think other men were hitting on his wife.

'You must be the cock-hungry bitch we're talking about,' he said crudely, in keeping with the direct approach he had

118

decided to adopt in the situation. The fact that neither of his hosts seemed shocked by his language was both encouraging and exciting.

Tammy was wearing a short black skirt beneath a white blouse and knee-high black leather boots. She was stunningly attractive, and fitted Oscar's description of her perfectly except she looked a lot younger than he had said she was. She was staring fixedly into the fire.

'Tammy,' David said firmly, forcing her to make eye contact with him. She was obviously finding it difficult to look at him. 'Tammy,' he repeated, asserting his control over her through her name, 'go and get me another beer while your husband tells me what a slut you've been.'

She opened her mouth as if to protest, but stopped herself.

Her rebelliousness and her reticence both appealed to David. He had not changed his opinion about her fidelity – in fact, he was almost positive now that she was being faithful to Oscar – and her obedience demonstrated a willingness to go along with her husband's wishes that pleased him. As she began taking his empty glass from him, careful not to let her fingers touch his, he held on to it waiting for her to look him in the eye again.

'Make sure it's a nice cold beer,' he said, telling her just how cold he wanted it with his tone.

She nodded, and walked quickly back through the living room towards the kitchen.

'Does she bring you a cream pie after her nights out?' he asked Oscar loudly enough for her to overhear. His question stopped her in her tracks for an instant, but it was not shocked offence David read in her body language. Observing her reaction, he made a mental note to the effect that she was either preparing cream pies for her little hubby to eat, or she liked the idea. He would have to find out which it was.

Tammy returned much sooner than David had expected her to with an ice-cold beer. She was plainly nervous and unsure of what to do next, so he helpfully pointed towards one of the large leather chairs close to his.

She was now seated directly in front of the fire across from him, her lovely features gilded by the soft glow of the flames. Her bare knees shone between her boots and her skirt, and both men studied them hungrily. Her skin was smooth and tinged with gold, and the tension in the room was now almost tangible. David was aware that Oscar was already beginning to sport an erection, and his wife was also becoming excited, seemingly against her will. Her breasts rose and fell quickly inside her shirt as she stared intently into the flames. When the stranger sitting in her living room abruptly rose from his seat, his motion startled her and she clenched her hands tightly in her lap.

David had spotted a drinks cabinet in an alcove and decided it was time to make himself feel at home. He paused as he walked by Tammy, and lightly rested one of his hands on her shoulder. 'Most of the whores I know like vodka,' he informed her, and felt her tremble ever so slightly. 'What would *you* like to drink?'

When she whispered, 'Vodka,' her husband moaned.

David poured himself a drink, and mixed Tammy's vodka with tonic and ice. He ignored Oscar completely. She took the glass from him, and accepted a cigarette with a polite, 'Thank you.' He sat down again and lit one for himself, once again ignoring her husband. He smoked and sipped his drink in silence for a minute, feeding off the submissive energy both the man and the young woman in the room were emanating.

'Cream pies,' he said finally. 'Do you think Oscar likes

them, Tammy?'

'I don't know,' she replied quietly.

'Let me put it another way. Has he ever tasted one?'

This time she refused to answer him.

David looked at her husband. 'You check her laundry basket for come stains and extra cream in case someone's been greasing her pussy?'

'I check, yes,' Oscar replied, sounding both ashamed and excited. 'I also check for traces of semen.'

'What about her cunt? Do you ever check up there? Do you ever bend her over the couch or the table and put your hand up inside her to see if she's been stretched out by some big cock, and to feel if she's been sprayed?' He saw Tammy cringing at this dirty talk, but he also noticed her suck passionately on her cigarette every time he said a crude word. Clearly, part of her loved it. 'Do you ever spread her when she gets home?' he went on. 'She's your wife, you know. Hell, you can strip the slut and spread her open any time you want to. You don't do that?'

Oscar shook his head.

'You've never pulled your fingers out of her snatch and found them covered in someone else's spunk?'

Oscar hung his head. His face was flushed red from the increasing pressure of his excitement, which came from facing his best and worst fantasies, no matter how shameful and sordid they were.

'The truth is,' David continued, enjoying himself immensely, 'you *want* to find her hosed down by some huge dick, but you're just too scared to own up to it. You want some rough man to hold her down and give it to her hard, because *you* can't.' He looked at Tammy again. 'Have you been out today?'

'N-no,' she stammered, 'I haven't.'

'You haven't been out anywhere at all?' David's voice was calm but demanding.

'Well, I – I went to the grocery store.'

'That's all the time you sluts need,' David said derisively. 'You've probably been riding some guy all afternoon. Now stand up and take your panties off. If your husband doesn't have the balls to check out your cunt, then I will.'

She looked at Oscar, but he stared back at her without expression. His mind was now locked on its own course, and she was not going to get any help from him.

'Get up,' David commanded again.

She hesitated another instant, before obeying him.

He reached out and ran his hands up the smooth skin of her thighs beneath her skirt to the top of her panties. He then pulled them all the way down her legs, and she stepped out of them quickly, almost as if she was afraid of tripping over them and falling into his arms. He then held the flimsy red satin in his hands for a moment before tossing it into the flames.

'Now spread them,' he said coldly.

Again she did as he instructed, and her husband looked on as another man's hand once more slipped up into her skirt and made its way to her pussy. David knew at once that she was as tight as a virgin, but he spent several minutes enjoying the warmth between her sex lips, and the fragrant juice flowing over his fingers told him she very much enjoyed his expert touch.

Finally, he slipped his hand out from beneath her skirt and told her to sit down again, but this time with her knees apart. She obeyed him, and he caught a brief glimpse of her neatly trimmed bush. Then he looked at her husband.

'She's been freshly stretched, Oscar.' It was not true at all, but David had no qualms about lying since he knew it was what they both secretly wanted him to do.

Tammy plucked her cigarette up out of the ashtray, and took a long drag from it before taking a quick sip of her vodka.

'Has your husband ever eaten a nice and creamy spunk-filled pussy pie you and your lover made for him?' David asked her, being intentionally crude to shock and unsettle them further.

Oscar was now surreptitiously rubbing his penis through his trousers while eagerly awaiting his wife's response.

'Yes, I have,' Tammy whispered. 'But Todd *makes* me do it.'

The answer took David by surprise, and made his penis stand at full attention as her unexpected frankness forced him to doubt his conviction concerning her innocence. Her performance as she sat straight-backed, almost primly, in the over-stuffed chair was either remarkably believable or she was telling the truth.

'Todd says Oscar deserves it for not being able to satisfy me.' She took another thirsty sip of her drink, and drew hard on her cigarette before blowing the smoke out rather like a pressure cooker finally letting off some steam. 'He loves to do me before sending me home, and he always makes sure I'm full of his come,' she embellished without need for further prompting from David.

'Do you give him head, Tammy?' he continued questioning her. 'Do you suck his prick and let him come in your mouth?'

She exhaled a long cloud of smoke in his direction, and nodded.

'Does he have a big, thick dick, Tammy?' he pressed bluntly. 'Is it so big you almost gag on him when you blow him?'

She nodded again, and yet her face remained beautifully expressionless as she drew on her cigarette.

'Do you want it, Tammy? Do you want his dick filling you up like you know your pathetic husband's can't?' David leaned forward in his chair towards her. 'Do you live for it, Tammy, live for the feel of his big hard cock stretching your pussy open and filling you up?'

She was now visibly trembling, as if David's words and dulcet tones were literally caressing her. She quickly stubbed her cigarette out in a crystal ashtray, set her glass down carefully beside it, and let her hand burrow into her lap almost as if it had a life of its own and she was powerless to stop it. But it was not an easy task reaching her clitoris through her skirt, and she bit her lip in frustration.

David looked across at Oscar. He was leaning his head back against the couch, and his rigid penis had found its way out of his trousers. He was stroking its modest dimensions slowly and intently while obviously imagining his beautiful young wife squatting over the huge hard-on he could never provide her with.

While the husband and wife team enjoyed their synchronised and fantasy-fuelled masturbation, David set his glass on the fireplace shelf, stood up, and pulled his own cock out of his pants.

Oscar was away in his own world, but Tammy immediately fixed her eyes on David's taught prick. She glanced across at her husband. All the dirty talk had gotten to her, and she was comparing sizes. Oscar lost without question. From now on, he always would.

David made his way to her, his penis rigid, the rift in his engorged head like a third eye staring blindly and rudely at her, because it did not see *her* personally; the only thing his erection cared about and wanted was her mouth and her pussy.

She took her eyes off it for an instant to look up at his face. Her expression was almost innocent in its excitement, as if some wondrous new game was being revealed to her that she was very much enjoying, but she was also looking to him like a child to an adult for guidance.

But there was to be no kind hand to guide her.

David was here to play a masterful role; a role he enjoyed playing very, very much.

He took hold of the base of his cock, and pulled back on the skin. The action had the effect of making his penis seem to grow even bigger, and made his helmet swell to almost painful proportions. With his other hand, he then took hold of her blonde hair and guided her mouth over his erection. She offered no resistance, and even used her free hand, the one not desperately stroking her pussy through her skirt, to cup his balls and squeeze them gently in time with his hips thrusting in her face.

On the couch, Oscar was in a trancelike state. His dreamy, slack-jawed stare seemed incapable of absorbing the reality of the act being performed by his wife with a strange man before his very eyes. The head of his small penis was almost purple from the pressure of the scene, and his hand's response to it. Somehow he managed to stem the impending explosion, and David was rather impressed by Oscar's control as he saw beads of perspiration meandering down the sides of the other man's face. He looked like an addict discovering the drug he had taken all his life was nothing compared to the intoxicating chemicals jumping along the synapses of his brain now like a firecracker in a crystal glass. They were shattering his preconceptions of pleasure with the sharp and painful picture – neatly framed by the tastefully decorated living room – of his wife obediently sucking another man's cock; a virtual stranger's cock.

After he had enjoyed her attentive mouth and tongue for a while, David took Tammy by the arm, pulled her roughly to her feet, led her over to a second couch, and shoved her down onto the plush cushions.

'Pull your skirt up,' he commanded.

She writhed enticingly as she struggled to obey him, pulling the material up around her waist and spreading her legs. Her neatly trimmed pussy was flushed a lovely rose colour, and glistening enticingly with her juices.

David stepped out of his shoes and trousers, knelt on the cushions between her knees, and lifted her legs up in the air, ready to penetrate her.

On the other side of the room, Oscar turned his head and saw his beautiful young wife spread-eagled and hungry for another man's cock. He sat up abruptly as a very real doubt flashed through his fantasy-fogged brain. He looked at David's rigid penis, resting flat up against his stomach, long and solid and much bigger than his own. He knew once the Englishman buried his pole in her pussy that Tammy would know what it was like to have a real erection inside her. She would know what it was like to really be filled and fulfilled. Shame, guilt and fear attacked his mind and his excitement ebbed, abruptly enabling him to think straight.

'Wait,' Oscar cried, 'I'm not so sure about this any more. I think I've made a big mistake.'

David had been expecting such a response at some point. So he had been sizing the man up since he stepped into his house, and he knew he could get the better of him if it came down to a fight. He hung Tammy's knees over his shoulders, so her pussy was almost obscenely exposed.

'Don't do it,' Oscar pleaded.

But David ignored him and lowered his cockhead towards Tammy's vulnerable pussy, and when she felt the head of his penis press against her opening, she moaned with longing. But before David enjoyed the pleasures of penetrating her, he watched her husband get up off the couch. As he did so, Oscar's trousers fell to his ankles and revealed his deflated prick. David looked at it before meeting his eyes. The man was scared. He had wanted to give Tammy a good time and watch her enjoy it, but he had made a big mistake. Oscar believed he was incapable of satisfying his wife, but he no longer wanted this proved to him. Now he was faced with another challenge. Could he fight for her? David thought not, even as he lowered Tammy's legs and stood up to face her husband.

Oscar looked intensely nervous and his penis had shrivelled pathetically. David, on the other hand, was confident, and his stiff rod was a testament to this fact.

'Please don't do it,' Oscar kept pleading with him. 'I don't think I can bear it.' But David merely laughed cruelly in his face.

'Sit down and enjoy the show,' he mocked. 'Your wife's now going to get the fucking she deserves.'

Oscar stepped defiantly forward, but David matched his stride, stopping him in his tracks. Oscar was almost in tears now, and he turned to his young wife for help.

But she offered him none. The extra tension of his anxiety, added to the prospect that she was about to be fucked by an attractive stranger while her husband was forced to watch, only intensified her excitement. She held her legs up and slipped two fingers into her pussy, working them slowly in and out, teasing both him and herself as she prepared to take the real thing.

'Don't let him do it Tammy, *please*,' Oscar begged. 'It's

all just a fantasy gone wrong. Let's work it out together, alone.'

'Just sit down and shut up,' she said frankly. 'I want his beautiful big dick up inside me and you're not stopping me. If you want me to stay with you, you'd better sit down and watch like a good boy.' She glanced down at his limp penis with contempt. 'You'd better get used to wanking that pathetic excuse for a prick, too, because from now on, I'm only fucking *real* men.'

Tears welled up in Oscar's eyes, and he sank down into the nearest chair.

Smiling, David returned to his position kneeling between Tammy's thighs.

'Fuck me hard,' she urged quietly, staring up into his eyes. 'You can do whatever you want to me as long as you fuck me hard.'

He leaned forward, and ripped open her blouse. She had full, round breasts set like lustrous pearls in a red satin demi-cup bra. David tugged it down and exposed her deliciously large, and achingly hard nipples. Then he turned his head to watch the torment on her husband's face as he massaged her breasts roughly, squeezing and moulding them between his fingers.

Despite his intense reservations, the sight of his young wife wantonly giving herself to an aggressive stranger transfixed Oscar. Full of fear, but desperate to save something for himself, he asked quietly and politely if David would at least consider wearing a condom.

'Not for a slut like her,' David replied, being intentionally brutal with his words. 'I'm going to plant my spunk deep inside her, and if you want it out, you can lick it out after I'm finished with her.'

'Oh, fuck me,' she begged, his obscene tirade nearly

sending her over the edge.

He obliged by bending her almost in half, leaning into her so her thighs were pressed against her breasts. In this position, David knew Oscar would have a good view of his cock ramming in and out of his wife's pussy.

Then he penetrated her at last, sinking deep inside her with one long insistent thrust.

Oscar never took his eyes off David's penis as it drove in and out of his wife. Even when her orgasms began flowing into each other and she begged David to come inside her, her husband did not look away. He watched for the fateful moment when the stranger's thrusts became more and more urgent, for the telltale sign of his buttocks tightening, which would signal the fact that his wife was passionately absorbing another man's seed.

Oscar saw the slight blissful grimace on the Englishman's face as he ejaculated deep inside his lovely Tammy, and then looked down at himself, and to his intense shame, Oscar realised that he, too, had come.

David and the other man's lovely young wife remained entwined for another five or so minutes, kissing and caressing each other as if they had been lovers for years. He had been happy with his performance, even before she told him he was the best fuck she'd ever had.

'I need a drink,' David announced, and Oscar's eyes went straight to his cock as he stood up. He was hoping to see evidence that this stranger, this foreigner, hadn't actually come inside his wife, but his hope was in vain; David's diminishing erection was gleaming with Tammy's juices and his own spent semen. Oscar groaned, planted his head in his hands, and shook it in despair.

When David returned with drinks for Tammy and himself, she was sitting up. He handed her the glass and sat across from her on a chair. He sipped his vodka contentedly for a moment, and then with his drink in his hand, he motioned for her to spread her legs again. She did as he instructed, and Oscar let out another anguished groan.

Tammy smiled smugly at David, and reached for a pack of cigarettes on the table beside her. She took one, and threw the pack to David.

He caught it. 'What do you think, Oscar?' he goaded. 'I made you a lovely cream pie just as you like them.'

'Thank our guest, darling,' Tammy said, adding insult to injury. 'He's left you a nice creamy pie for your supper, all soft and warm from the oven.' She drew on her cigarette, and then blew the smoke disdainfully across the room at him.

'Thank you,' Oscar whispered. 'Thank you very much.'

'Come on, sweetheart, you can do better than that,' she taunted him. 'It's a lovely pie. Look…' She lifted her bottom off the cushion and showed him her pussy. Her labia was as pink and shiny as the inside of a seashell, and it looked as though an ocean wave had broken against it and left its salty, glimmering foam behind as it ebbed.

Oscar groaned tormentedly yet again, and closed his eyes.

'The thing about cream pies,' David put in, 'is that if the husband doesn't eat it all up, the wife gets upset and feels compelled to make him another one. Do you get my drift?'

Oscar got his drift only too well; his face contorted in utter, blissful, unbearable torment.

'Come on, sweetheart,' Tammy urged callously, 'it's time for your supper. I know you want it; your little thing is sticking up again, and it never lies to me.'

'It's up to you, my man.' David smiled and blew smoke into Oscar's face, just as the man's wife had done. 'Get eating, or I'll have to bake her a fresh one. What's it going to be?'

Despite the battle going on in his head, Oscar's penis was clearly winning the war. It convinced him he had no choice but to lick Tammy's pussy clean of every last drop of another man's sperm; it wanted a piece of the pie, and any piece it could get.

And then to add insult to injury again, Tammy ordered Oscar to take his clothes off. She lit another cigarette while he undressed, got herself comfortable by propping cushions up on either side of her, and when she was ready, she motioned for her husband to get to work.

He sank to his knees before her, and began lapping away between her thighs. In this humiliating position his backside pointed directly at David. He was just the right distance away, his bottom was at just the right height, and David simply could not resist. So he lifted his feet and used the grovelling man as a footstool. It added to the other man's humiliation, but also, perversely, to the size of his dick.

'I always knew he was a pussy-whipped little wimp.' Tammy laughed down at her spouse, who kept right on licking her as eagerly as a dog. 'What do you think, he looks sort of natural down there, doesn't he?'

David nodded, and blew a thick stream of cigarette smoke between the cheeks of her husband's arse.

Oscar felt the smoky caress on his balls and his cock strained another notch, driving him to lap faster and deeper between Tammy's moist lips. The initial shock of the alien flavour had vanished and he found himself searching out her silky inner walls for every last drop of David's milk.

The pleasure of having her husband licking out another man's sperm was causing Tammy to experience the beginnings of another climax. It made her breathless as it slowly began breaking through her belly and over her sex.

'Harder,' she gasped. 'Get right up inside me and lick out every last drop. And while you're doing that, sweetheart, think about the fact that, from now on, I'm fucking any man I want to, including Todd.

'Yes, Todd *has* hit on me,' she revealed cruelly, intensifying her husband's torment, 'and now there's no need for me to turn him down. You'll be licking a fresh cream pie again in two days, as soon as I go back to work. And don't stop licking now, or I'll get Todd to butt fuck you like his sissy wimp.'

Oscar did not look as if he planned to stop what he was doing – licking Tammy's clit in a frenzy of lust. The couple appeared destined to come together, helped along by her increasingly foul mouth as she ground her pussy in his face.

'Lick it,' she said breathlessly. 'Lick it clean and get it ready for another load.' She put her hands behind his head and pulled his face hard against her. 'Your little prick won't even touch the sides now I've been stretched by a real cock… oh…' The memory of David's thick erection rising in and out between her slender thighs pushed her over the edge, and she screamed as her climax flooded her husband's mouth.

As she came down slowly, her body continued shivering in response to dozens of tiny aftershocks of pleasure that coursed through her young flesh in the most exquisite way imaginable. She looked across at David, and saw that his cock was as stiff as a pole again. Then she looked down at Oscar, still lapping away at her throbbing cleft. The night's events, and everything they had made her feel, had clarified all her fuzzy thinking about sex. As she looked down at her husband, and then across at David and his beautifully erect penis, she understood that there were different types of men in the world, and two of them were in the room with her. She was married to a submissive, insecure man who was happy to dine on the cream pie provided by a real man who had just given her the fuck of her life. And in that instant, she knew life was only going to get better and better.

Staring over at David's excitingly rigid penis, her eyes slowly worked their way up to his unsmiling face. She took a long, deep drag of her cigarette, held the smoke in her lungs for a moment, and then slowly exhaled as she reached across and stubbed it out in the nearest ashtray. David returned her gaze impassively, but lifted his feet off the other man's back as Oscar slumped to the floor, gripping his pulsing penis as he came all over himself yet again.

'I will be fucking David all night long in our bed,' Tammy informed him. 'Clean up this mess and then go to sleep on the couch. I'll call you when I need my pussy cleaned again.'

David awoke to the warmth of a woman's mouth and tongue worshipping his gentle morning erection. He gingerly lifted the quilt to watch Tammy's blonde head bobbing up and down beneath it.

'Well, good morning,' he said. 'Is this breakfast in bed?'

She looked up at him, and smiled. 'It's the only way to wake up, don't you think?' She promptly climbed over him, and guided his prepared cock up into her pussy. Then she sat up and rode him with a slow, steady rhythm while rubbing her clitoris with her fingertips.

David relaxed, and let the pretty young wife pleasure herself.

'I was a bit hard on poor Oscar last night,' she remarked breathlessly, turned on by the memory of how wicked she had been, 'but I got a little too carried away.'

'Where is he now?' David asked indifferently.

'Fixing breakfast – and a full English breakfast, just like

I told him to. I thought it might help you get your strength back,' she teased, and began riding him more urgently, biting her bottom lip as she selfishly drove herself towards another orgasm.

David grabbed a hold of her hips and ground himself gently but firmly between her legs, until he nearly reached his own peak. Then he urged her into a more relaxed rhythm to prolong the pleasure.

She leaned back and caressed her breasts, moulding their firm but tender flesh beneath her painted nails, and stretching her nipples to an almost obscene length.

Then their lovemaking was interrupted by a light knock on the bedroom door.

'What do you want?' Tammy demanded impatiently.

'Um, breakfast is ready, dear,' Oscar answered from beyond the closed door, sounding extremely tentative.

'Well, bring it in then,' she ordered.

Tammy remained proudly poised on her lover's cock, her back arched and her breasts thrust out defiantly as her husband entered the room. He was carrying a loaded tray, and he was naked. He walked to the bed and stood beside it, his eyes lowered as he awaited further instructions.

David paid the snivelling man no attention whatsoever; enrapt as he was with what the girl's clever vagina was doing to his cock.

'Put the tray over there, Oscar,' Tammy said without looking at him, 'on the dressing table.'

Oscar did as he was told. He placed the tray on the dressing table, and then turned back to torment himself with the sight of his wife's toned bottom moving up and down as she rode David's turgid erection with her pussy.

'Oh, not again,' Tammy murmured disdainfully as she gazed through hooded eyes over her shoulder and saw her husband's penis stiffening. 'Get out of here you dirty little man. Can't you see I'm with our guest and control yourself for once?'

For a moment it seemed Oscar was about to respond, but Tammy cut him off before he could utter a word. 'You must have some house chores to do,' she said scornfully. 'Well, go do them, and when David and I are finished here I'll be out to check on your work.'

Oscar left the bedroom without saying a word.

Aroused by her newfound power, Tammy braced herself on David's chest as she ground her pussy against him, and then she wailed in triumph as she came with his cock lodged as deep inside her as she could get it.

David was a man who knew how to please women, but he was also a firm believer in an alternative scenario to the one unfolding between Tammy and Oscar. On another occasion he would have put Tammy over the dresser, dipped her nipples in the hot egg yolks, and spanked her bottom until it was raw as punishment for taking her pleasure without the slightest thought for his own. But he recognised he was only a bit player in the drama unfolding in Rushmore Crescent, so he let the young woman have her fun. After all, he had enjoyed himself immensely already thanks to her and her pitiful husband. He respected the mysteries of human sexuality, and if Tammy and Oscar were happy playing this perverse little game, well then, he certainly had nothing against it. He did, however, intend to come himself, so he tightly held Tammy's waist and bucked up with his hips, driving his cock even deeper inside her.

'Looks like Oscar's getting another cream pie for breakfast,' he said through gritted teeth as he came.

Chapter Seven

David had seen it in countless movies and now there it was, the Golden Gate Bridge, one of the wonders of the modern world, and an embodiment of the American attitude that money and technology make anything possible.

He slowed down to enjoy his first sight of the bridge before he began his search for the restaurant where he had agreed to meet Donna. He was not a greedy man, but he sincerely hoped she was a member of the Frisco Swingers because she was looking for sex. The truth was, his exertions with Tammy had fed his desire rather than sated it. He pulled up at an intersection, and spotted the restaurant he was looking for half a block down the street.

David parked the RV behind the restaurant. Finding himself strangely nervous, he did not get out right away but instead remained sitting behind the wheel smoking a cigarette in an effort to relax.

Cars came and went, and he watched them impassively as he replayed last night's events in his head, and in doing so he found himself increasingly aroused and in the mood for gratifying sex. He was hoping Donna was not going to disappoint him, and remembered the caning he had given her in the *International Club* in Karachi, and once again wondered how the young teacher had finally managed to escape the place.

She was one of the first girls he had indulged himself with, and he found her reappearance in his life by way of a virtual newsgroup extremely intriguing. He wondered how she would feel about once again meeting a man who had beaten her, fucked her over a table in Pakistan, and then ignored her pleas for help. He wondered if she would remember him, and decided to let the meeting unfold without revealing his identity to see if she recognised him first.

It was a hot and sunny day and a number of diners were eating outside at tables cordoned off from the pavement by a velvet rope. One of these customers was Donna. David recognised her at once even though she had dispensed with the blonde curls. She had dyed her hair black and bobbed it, very much like a nineteen-twenties Flapper girl. Steeling himself for the encounter, he walked up to her table and introduced himself. She was wearing sunglasses, but she took them off and smiled up at him as she offered him her hand. It was only then that David paid any attention to the other girl sitting at the table with her.

'David, this is Kelly,' Donna introduced them, noticing him looking at her.

He sat down across from them.

'It's nice to meet you,' Donna continued politely. 'Are you in town for long?'

'No, just a few days,' he replied, both relieved and disappointed that she did not appear to recognise him – at least, not yet. 'It's nice to meet you, too.' He looked at Kelly and nodded to include her in this remark. He wondered if she knew why he was there. Surely she did, even though she had a delightfully naïve look about her.

A waiter appeared and Donna asked for a pitcher of water with lemon before sending him away again. While they waited for the water, the three of them perused their menus and commented on the light but tasty fare available. Talking about food broke the ice, and the atmosphere at the table quickly became pleasantly relaxed. The waiter returned with the water, and took their orders along with their menus. Then Donna asked David outright if he had ever used the Frisco newsgroup before to meet someone.

He was a little unsure how to reply, because Kelly's unexpected presence had put him on his guard.

'Oh, don't worry about Kelly,' Donna giggled, clearly sensing his discomfort, and her next statement shocked him even as it helped put him at ease again. 'She's here because she wants to be butt-fucked.'

'Donna!' Kelly gasped. 'Do you mind? I've only just met David.'

'Oh, not by you,' Donna added when she saw David's confused but hopeful expression. 'Of that you can be certain.'

Kelly was young, barely twenty-years-old by the look of her, and David was suddenly determined that her first experience with anal sex was going to include him, one way or another. He did not appreciate being teased.

'*Have* you met other people through the Frisco newsgroup?' Donna asked him again.

'I've met a couple of people, yes,' he replied, but did not volunteer any more information.

'Isn't it great?' she enthused. 'Likeminded people looking for a good time – what a civilised concept.'

'Well, it was certainly an interesting experience,' he agreed.

The waiter arrived with their lunch, and the conversation was interrupted for a while as they began eating. David used the time to study the very pretty Kelly. Her long blonde hair was cut in layers and she was wearing a sleeveless white dress that added to her innocent look. Her sunglasses were perched on top of her head and she sported several, obviously expensive, items of jewellery. She looked very much a wealthy West coast daddy's girl with her trim little waist that did not quite match the heavy fullness of her breasts. David suspected the presence of silicon, and lots of it.

'Do you like fucking strangers, David?' Donna asked him abruptly, successfully capturing his full attention yet again.

He deliberately made her wait for the answer. He motioned for the waiter, and ordered a shot of vodka. Then he looked Donna straight in the eye and said, 'I like fucking just about anyone, provided she's an attractive female.'

The two girls glanced at each other, and then giggled. Then Donna studied his face for a long moment and, as she did so, her brow furrowed and her expression changed. 'You know, you look a little familiar,' she said slowly. 'Is this your first trip to San Francisco?'

'Yes,' he answered, telling the absolute truth. He had no intention of dropping his guard until he discovered what Kelly's story was. She was obviously there for a reason, and he wanted to find out what it was before revealing his identity to Donna. 'What about you two?' he asked, moving the attention away from himself. 'Are you an item?'

'When we want to be,' Donna replied shortly.

'If the mood's right,' Kelly elaborated. 'Or if our husbands ask us to be.'

'You're both married?' David could not quite manage to conceal his surprise.

'Don't be so shocked,' Donna reproached him playfully. 'That's why we're in the group.'

'Your husbands don't mind?'

Donna laughed. 'Kelly's husband insisted on it. I mean, look at her.'

David was more than happy to oblige, and flashing him a beaming smile, Kelly straightened her back and proudly thrust out her over-developed breasts.

'But, I'm confused,' he said, at last managing to tear his eyes away from their spectacular beauty, much to the girls' amusement.

'Her husband's Rick Goldman.' Donna obviously thought she was clearing up the matter with such a brief statement.

David's face remained blank, his eyes unable to resist flickering back to Kelly's breasts every now and then.

'You know, Goldman Holdings, the real estate people?'

He shook his head. 'I said, I'm from out of town,' he reminded them.

'He's lovely, but he's seventy-three,' Kelly explained patiently.

'Oh…' David looked from her bright face to her mouth-watering breasts yet again. 'So I take it his love of figures extends no further than his bank account?'

Kelly smiled and shook her head. 'Oh no, he's as hungry now as he was when he was nineteen, I imagine, since obviously I wasn't even born then.' She giggled again at her own stupid statement. 'It's just that he likes me to have some fun with men my own age. He says I should get it every week, and so I do. He says that way I won't have an affair and leave him. The poor man, he's so silly.' She stretched her hands out in front of her and admired her massive diamond wedding ring, which was surrounded by an assortment of other more colourful precious gems. 'I would never leave my Rickie.'

Donna used her little finger to swipe away a crumb caught in one of Kelly's cute dimples. 'Want to see more of her?' she asked David, and he was beginning to feel rather shell-shocked by how quickly things were progressing.

Apparently, everything in America happened faster than anywhere else in the world.

As he hesitated and pondered the paradoxically vague but obvious offer, Donna groaned in mock despair. 'You really *are* from out of town, aren't you?' she mused.

The red Jaguar with the soft top belonged to Donna. David had noticed it earlier as he pulled into the parking lot and admired it. 'We'll take my car,' she announced.

The red leather was hot, and smelled new and expensive. Like the two girls riding in it, the Jaguar was designed to attract the eye.

'Where are we going?' David enquired, sitting up front with Donna while Kelly made herself comfortable in the backseat.

Donna slipped on her sunglasses. 'Downtown,' she answered briefly.

'"Where all the lights are bright",' he murmured tunelessly to himself.

'More like black,' Donna corrected him. '*Very* black indeed.'

Kelly leaned forward between the two front seats. 'And very fucking hard,' she added saucily.

Donna hit a button and the roof began spreading over them. David looked out of his side-window. They were entering what was obviously an unsavoury neighbourhood. He saw groups of youths sitting out on dilapidated porches, or tinkering beneath the hoods of old cars and blasting repetitive music. They sped through this depressing urban scene sitting comfortably inside a forty thousand dollar car.

'I take it Kelly's about to get her butt fucked,' David remarked with intentional frankness.

'Right on the button,' Donna said. 'Pun intended.'

141

'Your lover lives here, Kelly?' David asked, and both girls burst into delighted fits of giggling.

'Oh, how cute,' Kelly gasped when her amusement had subsided somewhat. 'Don't you just love the way the English speak? It's *so* sophisticated yet naïve.'

Donna furrowed her brow as she glanced again at the man sitting beside her. She seemed to be remembering something, but apparently she could not quite put her finger on what it was. 'It's a great accent,' she agreed, turning her attention back to the road as she slowed down. 'We're almost there, David. Don't lose your nerve in front of Wayne and Vince; they just like to intimidate people, and they're what Rickie likes for Kelly.'

'So that's what I get,' Kelly declared cheerfully.

The Jaguar only just missed the two posts holding up a tattered chain-link fence. Someone had decided to add a few more entrances with wire cutters, and Wayne, or perhaps Vince, had attempted to repair the damage with string.

'What's the deal?' David asked, feeling just a bit uncomfortable. 'I don't get it. What's going on?'

Donna pulled the Jaguar to a stop inside a carport that boasted what looked worryingly like a spray of bullet holes in the ceiling. 'Just enjoy the show,' she said jauntily. '*I* always do.'

The paint on the pinewood door was cracked and peeling, and in some patches was non-existent. It was immediately opened by a bald black man, well over six-feet tall, who ushered them into the house without a word. As they made their way down the corridor, the sound of the television grew louder and more insistent. It was tuned to a basketball game, and whether it was Wayne or Vince on the couch – and he was obviously the brother of the man who had opened the door – he did not deem it necessary to look up.

David had no idea what the rules of this strange scenario were, but he waited patiently while deliberately concentrating on the basketball game.

At last a commercial break released the seated man's concentration from the screen, and he deigned to turn his head their way. 'Who's the cave boy?' he asked laconically.

'He's a friend,' Donna replied, 'from out of town.'

'Pleasure to meet you,' David said. As the girls had warned him, he was indeed a little intimidated by the size of the two black men, who were both at least twenty years his junior, but he had been around the block a few times himself, and he managed to keep his nerves under control.

'Take a rock,' the basketball fan offered him a chair, and then looked at Kelly. 'There's a few six-packs in the cooler. I'm sure Mr Jig would like to chill out a bit before the main event.'

Just what the main event was David had not totally worked out yet. He knew it was sex, but when it was to take place, and in what form, appeared to hinge upon the length of the basketball game. He accepted the tin of beer from Kelly when she returned with it, and sincerely hoped that his hosts' team was winning.

When they all had their drinks in hand and were seated in a semi-circle around the television, Kelly slipped off the couch and knelt between the feet of the two black men. By now David had managed to distinguish Wayne from his brother by observing the single gold earring in his left lobe. Vince wore no earring.

For the next thirty minutes no one said a word. Wayne and Vince spoke quite eloquently with their actions, however. Whenever their side played badly, or the other side scored, one of them, and sometimes both of them, slapped Kelly. She cried out softly each time, but other than that the beautiful young rich girl made no protest.

As the game neared its conclusion the brothers became more passionate and more animated, and she responded by putting her arms around their legs. Occasionally she would run her hands over their tight jeans and caress their cocks through the denim, even though they slapped her for that, too.

David did not need to be a rocket scientist to work out the scenario sure to unfold once the game was over. He looked at Donna, and watched her hand sneak beneath the hem of her dress and make its way between her legs. She was attempting to be discreet, but if the atmosphere became much more intense he had little doubt her discretion would quickly go the way of Kelly's dignity.

Just then the intense but inanely pointless chatter of three studio pundits signalled the end of the game.

'Enjoy that, Mr Jig?' Vince asked him.

David was about to answer in the affirmative when Wayne suddenly shouted at Kelly. 'What you doing, you stupid girl? Can't you see the game's over and me and my friends are dry?'

Kelly looked around the room. Her cheeks were red from being slapped, and the way she was sitting – with her knees up against her breasts – gave David a tantalising glimpse of her white lace panties.

'Apologise to these people and get your ass in the kitchen,' Wayne ordered uncompromisingly, and Kelly did as she was told. Her demeanour had lost all the carefree confidence David had witnessed at the restaurant and during the drive downtown, as she disappeared into the kitchen.

Vince called after her and told her to get herself ready. 'We ain't got no time to be messing with you today, girl,' he said. 'We got some business to attend to.' He turned to Donna, who was silently, but rather obviously, squeezing her thighs together. 'And why are you here?' he demanded. 'You ain't due here for two days yet.'

'Rickie thought you could use the money,' she replied calmly. 'But if it's too much trouble for you boys, I mean, if you can't handle it twice a week, I'll take Kelly somewhere else.'

David did not consider this the wisest thing to say, and he could only hope Donna knew what she was doing.

'What do you mean, "*if* we can't handle it"?' Vince challenged. 'We could handle your little white ass fifty times a week if we wanted to.'

'Where the hell are those beers?' Wayne yelled. 'We're dying of thirst out here. Don't make me come in there and get them myself, girl.'

Some unusual sounds were coming from the kitchen, and David wondered what on earth Kelly was up to in there. But after a few minutes he found out when she walked back into the living room carrying a tray and wearing nothing except her lace panties, her bra, and white high-heeled sandals. Although she *was* wearing one more thing – a black leather dog collar with a leash that hung down between her breasts. The collar was dotted with silver studs that made it look dangerous, and contrasted erotically with her demure white undergarments.

Vince took his drink from the tray, and then slapped her hard on the bottom as she leaned over to offer the last beer to Wayne. She was wearing thong panties, and the black man's powerful blow left a clear handprint on her white cheek.

Wayne tugged her chain, and forced her down to her knees in front of him. 'Don't ever try to distract me when the

145

game's on,' he warned her. 'You're just lucky we won, or your ass would be on fire by now.' He unzipped his jeans, and an enormous cock that was still only semi-erect rose up towards her face. He slapped her again and she pulled back. 'What you doing?' he snapped. 'My cock ain't over there. Where you going?'

Vince laughed at his brother's treatment of the girl, and sipped his beer. For his part, David was enjoying the show too, and he kept his eyes trained on the lovely white girl now sucking a very big and very solid black cock. From the corner of his eye he discerned that Donna's hand had made it up into her dress, and she was obviously caressing her pussy through her panties. From what he could glimpse she appeared to be shaved, just as he remembered her. He turned his head away from Kelly's oral acrobatics – it did not seem possible she could get such an increasingly large penis into her dainty little mouth – and made eye contact with Donna. She almost seemed to be challenging him to say something, and the fact that he remained silent seemed to affect her. She moaned, and it became clear she was struggling to hold back an orgasm.

'Take it deep, girl,' Wayne ordered Kelly. 'Get it all the way down that sleek white throat of yours.'

He was ordering the girl to deep throat him, and Donna and David watched, mesmerised, as Kelly made an effort to obey him and nearly gagged.

By now Vince was also aroused, and his equally impressive cock was on display as he looked at Donna and stroked it pensively. 'You sure you don't want a black dick up your tight white ass, baby?'

'Rickie doesn't pay you to butt-fuck *me*,' she retorted breathlessly, ostensibly refusing the offer. 'I just like watching the show and making sure Mr Goldman gets his

146

money's worth.'

'But maybe we'll do you anyway, and Mr Jig here can sit back and watch two white girls get the shit fucked out of them by two big black men. Ain't that what he's here for?'

Donna did not appear at all worried by the threat. She slumped down on the couch, lifted her knees, and spread her legs to give Vince a clear view as she pulled the material of her panties to one side and exposed her shaved pussy. Then she made a play of wetting her index finger and sticking it up inside her. 'But maybe,' she purred, looking him straight in the eye, 'Mr Goldman will pull the plug on this sweet little deal you and your brother have here.'

For the first time David felt truly nervous. Vince was giving Donna an evil stare. He had one piece of lovely white ass spread out for his amusement, but such is human nature that he wanted the one denied him. The large man stood up in front of Donna. His cock was straining with desire and pointing angrily at her. He unbuckled his leather belt, and pulled it through the hoops without taking his eyes off her. Then he wrapped it slowly around his fist three times, and raised his hand. But when he brought the belt down again it was across Kelly's upturned bottom that it landed with a cruel smack. She squealed, yet she could do little to defend herself with Wayne's erection embedded in her mouth and throat.

'Fucking white whore,' Vince muttered, turning back to Donna. 'You get the fuck out of here before I lose my temper.'

'That's better,' she answered calmly, pulling her finger out of her pussy, which was wet and glistening with her juices. 'David and me will wait on the porch. Just make sure you fill her up good. Rickie likes her nice and slick when he bends her over his desk.' She got up off the couch, and smoothed down her dress. When she had composed herself, she picked up her beer and motioned for David to follow her out through the patio doors onto the back porch.

They settled down on two plastic chairs but kept the doors open so Donna could listen and make sure Mr Goldman was getting his money's worth. If that included his lovely young bride crying out beneath frequent cracks of a leather belt, and pleading not to have her ass fucked so hard, then he was getting good value for his money indeed.

Donna and David drank their beers and smoked a few cigarettes for the next hour or so while Kelly endured her weekly, and very exhaustive, ordeal. Occasionally, they heard her gasping, 'No, oh no, please,' but they also heard her screaming with pleasure as an orgasm ripped through her body, incontrovertible evidence of how much she was enjoying what the two big black men were doing to her.

Once David could not resist looking into the house – he would have preferred to remain inside and watch the action – and saw Kelly perched on an arm of the couch. Her bottom was hanging over the edge, and Vince had his erection thrust up inside it. Wayne stood in front of the couch, and she was leaning towards him bobbing her head up and down his black shaft for all she was worth. Vince made her work more difficult, however, by pulling her head up high with the dog leash. Then when Wayne was ready to come, he grabbed her head with one hand and pumped himself with the other as he shot his viscous spunk into her open mouth. Kelly swallowed hard as he fired into her, and continued to suck him hungrily, until he grunted and nudged her head, and made it clear he wanted her to stop. He slipped his sensitive prick from between her pouting lips, and slapped her again, this time with his penis. He used it like a semisoft truncheon, slapping her on one cheek and then the other while she chased the still thick and impressive tool hoping to get another taste of it.

'You white sluts just love dark meat, don't you?' he taunted her, and she nodded and moaned shamelessly. 'Show me how much you love being a black man's whore,' he said and, turning around, shoved his ass towards her.

She reacted by immediately pushing her face between his muscled buttocks and eagerly thrusting her tongue into his sphincter.

David smiled at the scene, and watched for a few more seconds before turning reluctantly back to Donna. She was sipping a fresh beer, and watching some kids playing basketball in a court cordoned off with steel fencing. 'Wayne just shot his load,' he casually informed her.

She glanced at her watch. 'Four o'clock,' she observed. 'Just Vince to go, and then I'll get Kelly home before Rickie gets back from the office.'

David resumed his seat as Kelly's moans of ecstasy continued to emanate from the living room, accompanied by a stream of obscenities as Vince followed his brother and also shot his load into her.

'What's the deal,' David asked his attractive companion, 'with you and Kelly and this husband of hers?'

'You could call me a moderator, or a mediator,' Donna told him. 'Some of our members call me "the go between".'

David was interested in what she was telling him, and let her see it.

'I hooked up with a number of people on the newsgroup,' she explained. 'You see, there are a lot of crazy people out there, and it's all about trust. I gave a few parties, brought a few people together, including Kelly and Rickie, and now I guess I just do this sort of thing most of the time.'

149

'Do you work?' he asked. 'A real job, I mean.'

'You saw those two,' she answered. 'What does it look like? I've got to spend time checking them out, making sure they're not on drugs or dealing drugs, making sure they don't have any diseases. It's a fulltime job, believe me.'

'And you have to know just how far to push them to get what you want,' David elaborated. 'I was very impressed with you in there.'

She was somewhat taken aback by the fact that he knew just what she had been doing by riling Vince and Wayne earlier, and her eyes narrowed as she stared at his face, clearly still trying to place it.

'Does it come naturally?' he went on questioning her, wondering if the moment would come when she finally recognised him. 'Or did you learn it from somewhere?'

She looked at him even more intently. 'I picked up some techniques,' she replied slowly, 'and learned the rest by myself.'

David was about to ask Donna where she had learned so much when Wayne called for her to get the white bitch out of his house. So she and David got up, and returned to the living room to find Kelly bent face down over the back of the couch.

'Where's our money?' Wayne demanded.

'Now boys, you know the rules,' Donna said patiently. 'First I get to check the workmanship, and *then* you get paid. It's just like working at a construction site. Think of me as your foreman.' She stepped up to Kelly but she was looking at Vince. 'Open her up for me, if you please.'

He flashed her a look of contempt before he reached out to grip Kelly's buttocks, and spread them open.

'There you go.' David thought Donna's tone was

150

dangerously patronising. 'That wasn't so difficult, now was it?'

'Just hand over the money,' Wayne cut in. 'We've got places to be.'

'Patience is a virtue, and first I have to make sure you boys haven't been where you're not supposed to go.' She slipped the whole of her index finger into her mouth, drew it slowly and provocatively out again, and held it up in front of the scowling brothers.

'We plugged her ass, that's all,' Vince insisted, 'same as always. Do we have to go through this shit every time?'

Rather ceremoniously, Donna pushed her index finger up inside Kelly's pussy. She held it there for a few moments, infuriating Wayne and Vince and especially the latter, who was still holding Kelly's bottom cheeks open. After a pensive moment Donna withdrew her digit and held it up to the light, where she rubbed a fine oily film between her thumb and forefinger. 'Hmm…' she pondered, 'what do you think?' She turned to David. 'Have these two boys been in the honey pot?'

Despite being wary about the seemingly volatile situation he had found himself in, David was excited by the fact that he was finally going to get to touch Kelly himself. He had been enormously envious of the two brothers who had gotten to fuck her lovely bottom and come deep in her mouth, while he made do with a tin of beer and a neighbourhood basketball game. So he stepped forward and, foregoing Donna's dramatics, slid two fingers into Kelly's receptive pussy. She was understandably moist, but she was also relatively tight, and he reached the same conclusion that he guessed Donna already had reached.

'No, I don't think they've been in the honey pot,' he announced, reluctantly pulling his fingers back out of the temptingly compliant young woman.

'You're sure she's intact, David?' Donna asked him soberly, and when he nodded, she smiled. 'Good, I thought so, too.' She then opened her purse and handed the brothers their money while Kelly straightened up, and returned to the kitchen for her clothes. Within minutes she was dressed just as she had been before, and looking every inch the pride of the tennis club.

When the three of them were alone again in Donna's Jaguar, Kelly again leaned into the front seat just like an excited child. 'Christ, David,' she said, 'I don't know if it was you being there, but Wayne and Vince gave me the best butt-fuck ever!'

'I think you can thank Donna's subtle manipulations for that,' he replied. 'She's a clever girl. She had full control of Wayne and Vince just with her words. She knew just how far to go, and when to back off.'

'I'm flattered,' Donna said coolly. 'You seem to know a bit about control yourself. Does it come naturally, or did you learn it?' she echoed his earlier question.

'I picked it up when I was around Malibu beach,' he told her. 'Ever been to Malibu beach, Donna?'

Kelly shrieked and had to brace herself desperately to avoid being flung towards the dash as Donna suddenly slammed her foot down on the break pedal, bring the car to an abrupt halt. 'What the hell…?!' she gasped, but her voice trailed away when she saw the look of horror on her friend's face. She glanced at David for some clue as to what was going on, but his eyes were fixed on Donna's expression.

Donna's heart was pounding in her chest. The horrors of the *International Club* were all flooding back to her as she looked deep into David's eyes, searching out his intentions.

'I knew I knew you,' she whispered, stalling for time. 'Your voice… I just couldn't recall when and where, but I knew I knew you.'

David was enjoying her agitated state, even though he had no ill intentions. 'How did you escape?' he asked her, genuinely curious.

'Escape?' Kelly echoed. 'What the fuck is he…?' but her voice trailed away again. Donna had told her about her experiences in Pakistan, and she abruptly realised that must be where David and her friend had met.

A car sounded its horn at them, but it took David's voice to get Donna to react. 'You're blocking traffic,' he pointed out gently.

'Sorry?' she looked at him blankly, obviously seeing another place and another time, not the highway ahead.

'You're blocking traffic,' he repeated patiently, gratified by her reaction.

She started, and floored the accelerator, sending Kelly plunging into the backseat. 'Where are we going?' Donna asked faintly.

'I thought we were taking Kelly home,' David answered, surprised by the question.

'No,' Kelly objected. 'I thought we were taking you back to the restaurant so you could pick up your van. Isn't that what we agreed on, Donna?' She was making an endearing effort to protect her friend from a man who was clearly upsetting her.

Despite how much fun he was having, David decided it was time to take control of the situation. It was obvious Donna was frightened and needed to be reassured. 'Pull in,' he directed her, 'over there, in front of that bar. I'm not ordering you to stop; I just think it would be a good idea if you let me buy you a drink. I'm sorry, this is all my fault, I should have said something earlier.'

'Okay,' Donna murmured without looking at him, keeping her eyes fixed carefully on the road, 'you can buy me a drink.'

'Three whiskies,' David said to the barman. 'Large ones.'

They sat at a table beside a window overlooking the street.

'You're a bastard,' Donna finally broke the tense silence after she took her first sip of whisky. 'I begged you to help me, and all you did was fuck me stupid and then leave me to rot with Javed and that horrible midget.'

'What could I do?' David asked reasonably. 'Did you ever hear me say I was brave? Do you think I could have busted you out of there like it was some movie, or something? I was scared too, you know.'

'Not too scared to beat me with that cane and stick your prick up me whenever you felt like it.'

'It would have been someone else's prick if it wasn't mine.' He assumed she had naturally preferred his.

'I take it you two have met before,' Kelly cut in sarcastically. She clearly found David's measured tones and polite manner reassuring, although she had lived in San Francisco long enough to know they did not guarantee quality of character, or even sanity, for that matter.

Donna turned to her friend. 'Remember when I came back from Karachi and I told you about what happened to me in that club?'

Kelly nodded. 'Of course I do. How could I ever forget?'

'And remember I told you about the time this so-called English gentleman came in and I thought I was going to be rescued at last?' Kelly nodded. 'Well, this is him.'

'That was *you*?' Kelly sounded more intrigued than outraged. 'And you've been tracking her down all this time?' She seemed to find the concept quite romantic.

'Wait a minute,' David said quickly, 'I haven't been tracking anyone down at all. Stalking may be an American pastime, but this was just coincidence.'

'What?!' Donna exclaimed. 'You're saying it's a complete coincidence you ended up here in San Francisco in a bar with me? That's some fucking coincidence, I must say.'

'Do you know how long it's been since I saw you in Karachi?' he asked her patiently. 'It's been years. I've been halfway around the world since then, living in some hut in Russia freezing my balls off. And, I hate to say it, but you were the last thing on my mind.'

'In Russia?' Kelly sounded even more interested. 'What were you doing in Russia?'

'It's a long story,' he replied dismissively. 'Let's just say that people were after me. I've only just got it all sorted out, and now I'm on my way to Miami. I bought a laptop computer to beat the boredom of the road by surfing the Net, and I just happened to come across the Frisco Swingers.'

'And you saw my ad?' Donna asked. She sounded calmer, as though she was beginning to believe him.

'Who didn't?' He laughed in an attempt to lighten the mood. 'I recognised your smile at once, and I couldn't resist calling you.'

'As I recall,' Donna said pointedly, 'I wasn't doing much smiling the last time you saw me.' For a moment she seemed about to keep up the 'I'm hurt' attitude but then, suddenly, she smiled. Kelly smiled too, as if she had been waiting for her friend's permission to do so, and David's relieved grin completed the circle.

'I'll get us some more drinks,' Kelly offered. 'But don't

say anything more until I get back. I want to hear it all.'

David and Donna sat in silence while she was gone, avoiding each other's eyes by gazing over at the bar. Fortunately, Kelly was back in less than a minute.

'Okay, I'm ready now,' she said eagerly.

'So, *how* did you manage to get away from Khan?' David asked Donna again.

She held up her left hand, displaying a row of expensive rings. 'Khan had a party, and along came Doug.' She wiggled her wedding finger. 'There were a lot of businessmen on the yacht, and a lot of girls. Khan had extra girls brought out from the club, and we were told to entertain the guests. When I realised how wealthy Doug was, I was determined to give him the best blowjob of his life followed by the best fuck of his life. I did, and they worked like a charm. He fell in love with me and asked Khan if he could buy out my contract. Khan asked a ridiculous amount for me,' she lowered her hand while gazing at the large diamond adorning her gold wedding band, 'but love shone through.'

'Quite a romantic story, isn't it?' Kelly declared.

'I have to admit, when I saw that film of you and the Japanese guy on the boat,' David said quietly, 'I thought you were dead. It was quite a wonderful shock seeing you on that newsgroup.'

'I could have you arrested, you know,' Donna informed him. 'I could have you thrown in jail for what you did to me back there.'

'But you won't,' David assured her placidly, before changing the subject slightly to take her mind away from such an action. 'So what happened when you got back home? Did life get a little boring for you? Did you miss all the sex and all the attention? And Khan threw exciting parties; your life ended up being quite different from the one you had expected as a teacher, when you set out with the high moral ideal of helping bring a little civilisation to the natives.'

Donna laughed, and finished her second drink. 'That's one lesson I learned for sure, to leave people alone and let them live however they want to, and believe whatever they want to.' She pushed her chair back, and stood up. 'That's why I do the swingers scene here, because it's for people who want pleasure but also just want to be left alone. Now let's get going before these drinks get to me. I've got to get Kelly home safe and sound.'

Chapter Eight

Kelly's husband bought and sold real estate, and by the look of their home, he had kept the best property for himself. The house was Italianate, white and imposing, and made a definite statement about the pleasures of wealth from its hillside pulpit.

Donna waited for the electronic gates to swing smoothly open before driving her Jaguar slowly and respectfully up the stone cobbled drive to the carport, in which a red Mercedes convertible sat in polished splendour shaded by the marble-faced sandstone. David, who had gone back for his RV, followed her through the gates, but parked outside the carport.

'Nice piece of architecture,' he said to Kelly when they met again beside the Jaguar. 'It lacks the personal touch of Wayne and Vince's place, but it has its merits.'

'It's the bullet holes,' she declared, 'I should have my designer put some in for effect.' She reached in to the backseat of the car and picked up her jacket, which she threw jauntily over her shoulder. 'Wayne and Vince supply a service for my husband, and that's how I think of them, as servants.'

The entrance hall was a riot of colour created by sunlight streaming into the large space through a stained glass window above the entrance, and through glass-panelled doors. David paused to enjoy the warmth, and to watch luminous colours playing their way up the sweeping staircase.

'Drinks, anyone?' Donna called from a room adjoining the hall.

He turned towards her voice. 'Please,' he said, but then stopped again to admire the colourful play of light. He was remembering his time in the tundra and how the snow and ice sometimes split the light into dazzling spectrums very similar to the ones before him now.

The inviting clink of glasses eventually drew him into the room, and he asked Donna to pour him some vodka. She was standing before an antique bar set between two French doors covered by transparent white curtains.

'Don't tell me,' Kelly said from where she reclined on a dark leather Chesterfield, 'a martini, shaken, not stirred.'

David went to collect his drink. 'We share similar tastes in many things,' he said, 'but we do differ on how to take our vodka. Just tonic please, Donna... thank you.' He seated himself in a wingback chair, and looked up at a large portrait of a man. 'Rickie?'

'Yes.' Kelly got up to collect her bourbon, and then went and stood beneath the painting. 'Handsome, isn't he?' she gazed admiringly up at her husband.

'I thought his most endearing quality was money,' David remarked cynically, deliberately baiting the rich young woman he had just seen fucked up the ass by a poor black man.

'*Lots* of money,' Donna corrected him.

Kelly continued gazing up at her husband's portrait in a seemingly genuine display of wifely pride and affection. 'He's strong... he's powerful.' She glanced at David before returning her attention to the portrait. 'That's what really makes a man, isn't it, how strong and powerful he is?'

'Definitely,' he agreed. 'In my experience most women prefer men with power, and power usually, if not always, means money. What women love to feel is a man's power, and wealth certainly constitutes power in our society. Women also appreciate the security it offers.'

Kelly and Donna glanced at each other.

'Will I be meeting him?' David asked.

Donna stared out through the French doors. 'Actually, he's pulling up right now,' she announced.

David caught a glimpse of a burgundy Rolls Royce as it turned the corner in the direction of the carport. He sipped his drink, and abruptly realised he was feeling tense. A quick glance at Kelly and Donna convinced him that they, too, were on edge, although not in a negative way. They made him think of little girls waiting on their favourite uncle who always arrived with a pocket full of exciting treats.

Rick Goldman took his usual side entrance into the house, and in so doing startled David with his sudden appearance. For a seventy-something man, he was in remarkably good condition. He noticed David immediately but paid him no attention, and he also ignored Donna. His eyes, alight with happiness, were fixed on Kelly.

A man should enjoy all his possessions, David thought with a touch of envy.

Kelly approached her husband, and bent her right leg up behind her as she reached up to kiss him on the lips. He smiled down at her, and then stepped behind a large mahogany desk as she moved over to the bar to fix him a drink. By the time she set a glass containing an inch of tawny bourbon in front of him, he was clipping the end off a cigar. He put it in his mouth and waited for her to light it, which she promptly did. After several puffs the cigar was lit evenly, and Kelly had opened a silver cigarette case. She extracted an unusually long and slender cigarette, lit it, and leaned casually back against the desk.

'Has she been to see her friends?' Rick Goldman finally spoke, in a deep, slightly hoarse voice. The question was directed at Donna.

'Yes sir, and both boys drilled her good.'

Kelly moved to stand between her husband and the desk with her back to him. 'Butt only, as always,' she said.

Rick finally acknowledged David by fixing him with a piercing stare.

'David,' Donna said by way of a simple introduction. 'He's a friend. We took him with us to the boys' place earlier.'

Rick knitted his eyebrows as if weighing some great question in his mind. Then he drank his bourbon down in a single gulp, thrust the cigar back in his mouth, got up, walked around the desk, and pushed Kelly forward across it with one hand. 'Well, no time like the present,' he grumbled to no one in particular as he lifted the hem of her white dress, and sought out her panties. With two firm tugs the flimsy lace material came away in his hand.

As Kelly rested calmly on her elbows, her husband pulled the cigar out his mouth and held the torn panties up to his face. The heavy smell of tobacco mingling with the subtle but equally potent scent of fresh sex sent the blood pumping into his old cock. The wiry old guy impressed David with the solid tool he pulled out of his pants, and Kelly fell forward beneath his first thrust.

The room was utterly silent as Rick stabbed his wife's pussy with long swift strokes while David and Donna looked on, and Kelly herself puffed nonchalantly on her cigarette. Her husband made small, rather helpless sounds as he worked his way towards an orgasm, which came quickly enough as he pushed deep into her pussy with one

161

final urgent motion. The release of his seed seemed to exorcise all the tension from his body, and his features took on a more kindly expression. While the last tremors of sexual pleasure subsided, the old man drew deeply on his cigar as Kelly remained casually smoking over the desk, and David admired her expensive cleavage. Then the real estate tycoon looked down at his deflated cock as it snaked its way out of his young wife. He appeared faintly troubled as he glanced over at Donna, and for a moment she looked back at him in confusion before suddenly springing forward.

'Here,' she said, 'let me.' She took her friend's torn panties in one hand, Rick's cock in the other, and proceeded to wipe him clean.

'Be with you in a moment,' Rick suddenly and unexpectedly said to David.

'No rush, take your time,' he replied, thinking the whole scene was somewhat surreal. He did not know if his first words to the multimillionaire sounded sarcastic but he had gotten into the habit of saying whatever came into his head. His reaction now bothered him, as he had never been overly impressed by wealth.

Donna gave Rick's cock a final wipe and a quick kiss before she dropped the torn panties into the wastepaper basket.

As he watched her little performance, David abruptly realised what was making him anxious. He *was* impressed by the man, although not just his wealth. He was impressed with Rick Goldman himself, with his body, his perverse mind, his possessions and his confidence. David had not really considered his own age until now, not in any deep, meaningful sense. Here, however, was the living embodiment of what he hoped for in his own autumnal years.

162

Rick gave his wife's bottom a playful but firm slap, told her to go get showered and changed, and she and Donna promptly left the room together.

'The accent sounds English,' Rick commented once they were alone.

'It is,' David replied.

'A bit far from home, aren't you? Doing a bit of travelling?'

'You could say that.'

'You turn up at a strange home with two beautiful women, one of whom calls you a friend although she's never mentioned you before, a woman who just took you to watch my wife get drilled by two black studs, and you sit there as cool as a cucumber while she gets it again from me, this time in the right hole.' He pointed at David with his cigar. 'I think we got ourselves an enigma here.'

The distinguished elderly man moved towards a door, and motioned for his guest to follow him into a room with a stunning view of the valley. The centrepiece of the games room was a snooker table covered with purple baize. There were numerous chairs scattered around the marble floor, and a white grand piano sat near one wall next to a row of French doors. Numerous mirrors reflected the sunlight streaming into the large space, and a row of lights hung over the table.

'It's a beautiful room,' David commented.

Between each door rose marble columns on which sat the busts of various Roman emperors. The highly polished pedestals were infused with streaks of amethyst, but each bust was snow-white.

'Do you like snooker, David?' Rick asked.

'Yes, I do. I've never seen a purple baize before, though.'

'It's one of the few English games I care for. That cricket

game of yours, does anything ever happen? How long does it last, a couple of days, I hear?'

'Five,' said David, 'if it's a test match.'

'Well, let's play a game of snooker and you can tell me how you came to be at my wife's weekly servicing. I'm not used to others knowing so much about me before I've even been introduced. I like to be the one holding the cards, if you know what I mean.'

David returned Caesar's suspicious stare. 'I can see that,' he said.

'You set up, and I'll pour us some more drinks.' Rick held his glass up inquisitively.

'Vodka,' David told him, 'and a little tonic, please.'

Rick handed David his drink, and played the first shot.

'If I tell you how I met Donna, will you answer a question for me?' David asked his host as the game got underway.

'Shoot.'

'Why do you do it?'

'Send Kelly to the ream machines, you mean?'

David nodded.

'Korea,' came the ambiguous reply. 'I was in Pusan when the Chinese and the North Koreans turned up to take the city. I watched thousands of people die over a piece of real estate, and something inside me clicked. So when I got out of the army I set up this business, and for forty years I fought hard to make this company what it is today. I can have any woman I want, believe me. Young, beautiful, even intelligent women would all open their legs for me on account of my money.'

'So, sending Kelly to be butt-fucked every week by a couple of black studs is a test of her love?'

'Don't know about that,' the old man replied seriously.

'Hell, every guy in the golf club has a young wife who swears love and undying loyalty to him. Yet the moment he croaks, she's off with some young gun, and her millions.' He puffed on his cigar, and said no more until he'd finished a good thirty-four break.

'We all see it, all of us rich old men,' he continued, screwing some chalk onto his cue tip. 'We see it happening to our friends around us, and we look at our young wives working on their swing with one of the young and handsome club pros, and we wonder. We wonder if he's plugging her, or whether they're just waiting for her hubby to keel over before they sail off into the sunset with her. But you can't give it up, not that beautiful trophy with the bouncing breasts and the big doe eyes.'

'It's a punishment then; that's why you send Kelly to Vince and Wayne every week?' David said, trying to understand.

'Not a punishment, no.' Rick took his turn at the table again. 'It's just that Kelly has to go to Pusan. She's got to hear the shells and see the bodies. She's got to work for her money just like I did. Hell, I don't know if that girl loves me or if she's waiting just like all the other young wives for me to kick the bucket, as they say.' He took a long drag on his cigar, which was still going strong, and thought for a moment.

'All I want is to know that when I'm gone, she's worked hard for her money and deserves it. Then I couldn't care less what she thinks of me. She keeps me happy and does whatever I tell her to. I got another twenty years, thirty tops. I can't imagine the last few being too active, though. By then Kelly will be, what… fifty? By the time she's got her hands on my money, she'll have earned every last nickel.'

There was logic in there somewhere, David thought, as his eyes met Caligula's baleful stare.

For the next two games, both of which Rick won, David outlined his relationship with Donna; how he had met her at the *International Club* in Karachi after fleeing the Afghan Russian war, and how he could do little to help her escape from the kidnappers who made her work at the club by sexually serving men from all over the world.

His host showed little interest in David's Afghanistan adventure. His attention was piqued only when David mentioned what went on in the club, and what he had done to Donna.

'That explains a lot about her,' Rick mused. 'Her husband owns a construction company and he does a lot of work for me. We had dinner a few times, and I always thought she was a firecracker. You can tell, can't you, the body language, the flirting. I love the way she keeps that hair in a neat little bob. Love the colour, too.'

'But I thought the girls sometimes did a little thing for you,' David risked stating matter-of-factly.

'Yes, so?'

'Well, she's a blonde, isn't she, Donna? I thought you would have spotted that right away when the girls do whatever it is they do for you.'

'Wouldn't know.' Again Rick chalked the tip of his cue, and blew away the excess powder. 'She keeps it shaved. Always looks as smooth as that snooker ball when I see it.'

David realised then that he had never actually seen Donna's pubic hair either. The *International Club* employed a huge brute of a man called Javed to train the girls. It was also his job to shave them, and to keep them that way. Like him, Rick obviously preferred a woman's smoothly shaved

166

pussy, but Easterners positively insisted upon it.

'She was shaved back then too, come to think of it,' he said, thinking out loud, 'but as I recall, she had beautiful blonde hair...'

'You two boys getting along?' Kelly asked as she suddenly swept into the room, with Donna following close behind her.

Rick looked up from the table, and smiled. 'I see you two have something planned,' he observed, and David thought so himself. Both girls were wearing Merry Widows with stockings. Donna's outfit was white and Kelly's was black. They were freshly made-up, and both strode confidently across the marble floor in extreme high-heels whose colour matched their lingerie. Kelly sauntered over to David and liberated his glass as Donna did the same with Rick's drink.

'I think we're all in need of some new refreshments,' Donna declared in a seductive tone. The girls also fancied a smoke, for once everyone had a new drink in hand, they each took a long cigar from a large mahogany humidor, and lit up.

'Oh, can we play?' Kelly pleaded in what struck David as a deliberately coquettish tone.

Donna stroked her fingers under Rick's chin. 'We want some afternoon fun, Rickie,' she purred. 'Can we go to our special room and play some games?'

David watched, mesmerised. The girls looked absolutely stunning, and his head was spinning from all the fine vodka he was drinking. He had also accepted the Cuban cigar Kelly offered him, and he was definitely all for some afternoon fun himself.

'What the hell,' Rick gave in without a fight. 'If a man can't have a little fun after work, what's the world coming to.' He deliberately sank the white ball, and then he and the girls quickly swept those remaining on the table into the pockets.

David was intrigued, and his interest sharpened when Rick moved his hand beneath the table and pressed a button. A low electric hum told David something was about to happen, and he noticed the purple cloth slowly sliding towards one end of the table to reveal a slab of polished slate, which abruptly dropped away in two pieces. It was so perfectly made, he had not even noticed the join running lengthways down the centre of the table.

He looked at his host, who smiled at him. The girls also seemed to be enjoying the puzzled look on David's face as Rick stepped forward, and reached over the part of the table furthest away from the gathered purple baize. He was releasing a catch, and when it clicked, he pulled the cushion forward and the end of the table opened up like a gate. They were all now faced with what looked like the entrance to a subterranean mausoleum. The fallen slate of the table created the sides of a steep staircase leading down to a set of copper doors.

'That's one hell of a cellar,' David remarked, seriously impressed.

'Isn't it just?' Rick gestured for him to start down the steps, and the girls followed behind them. David reached the doors first, but they were locked, and while he waited for Rick to extricate the key from his pocket, he studied the swirling designs in the copper. Like the girls, he was growing increasingly excited.

'Here it is,' his host declared when he finally found the key. 'I always keep it on me. We don't want any strangers stumbling into our little fun room, now do we?'

As the girls giggled their agreement the key entered the

hole it had been made for, and the bolt ground its way back into the lock. Rick then turned the circular handles, and pushed. The doors opened silently and smoothly, but nothing was visible beyond them. The room remained in absolute darkness until its owner stepped forward, and then suddenly two cone-shaped containers came alive with real flames.

'Sensors,' the millionaire explained of the unasked question. 'It adds a real touch of magic.'

The four of them entered an antechamber, and in the flickering firelight David made out walls colourfully decorated with hieroglyphs and smiling, life-size Egyptian deities.

About eight feet in front of them, another set of doors blocked their passage. These needed no key, however. Rick pushed them casually open to reveal a large room already lit by flames dancing inside more copper cones. Directly in front of them was a gilded throne, and all around them ancient Egyptian relics were on display.

For a moment David forgot the two beautiful women in lingerie as he stepped into the eerily lit room, and began studying the artefacts. He picked up a small figurine of a Nubian soldier holding a spear. It felt heavy in his hand, and looked old. 'This is a very fine display,' he said cautiously.

'It's more than that,' his host declared proudly, 'it's a museum.'

David could scarcely believe what the man was saying. 'You mean, all these pieces are genuine?' he said.

'The real McCoy,' Rick beamed at him. 'Everything in here has been verified by one of the highest authorities on ancient Egypt.'

'How?' David asked in wonder, genuinely interested in the subject. 'There are millions of copies out there, and very good ones, too. How can you be so sure all these pieces are real?'

'Let's just say we have a friend who visits Kelly when we're getting ready to buy another piece.'

David looked at Kelly, who was smiling alluringly.

'We value his opinion,' Rick added, 'and Kelly values his cock. It's quite an impressive tool for an old archaeologist. He's one of the pre-eminent authorities on ancient Egypt in this country. The man knows his stuff.' He chuckled. 'He knows Kelly, too. Doesn't he, sweetheart?'

Kelly giggled, and Rick told her to go fetch them all a drink.

David watched in growing fascination as Donna and Kelly each picked up a golden cup, and held it beneath the open mouth of a carved crocodile. A dark-golden fluid immediately ran out of the animal's toothy jaws into the goblets, and the two girls then brought the mysterious offering over to the men, and all four tasted it.

'Mm, that's very sweet,' David commented. 'But very nice.'

'It's date wine,' Kelly informed him, 'made from a recipe found on the walls of a prince's tomb.'

Rick laughed, and seated himself on the throne. On a table beside it sat two statues of black cats facing each other. He passed his hand between them and music – quiet but evocative and rich with sensual rhythms and percussion – filled the room.

'More sensors?' David asked.

'Light sensitive,' Rick explained, 'drilled into the eyes. Don't worry, these two aren't ancient artefacts.' He motioned for his guest to make himself comfortable on a long couch near the throne, and when the girls began dancing for them, David realised he was watching a well-practiced ritual his host undoubtedly enjoyed on a regular basis.

The music never stopped; it went on relentlessly, perfectly balanced between high and low notes, and the girls continued translating its haunting melodies into smooth undulating motions that brought them closer and closer together in a slow, erotic dance.

David glanced at Rick's benevolent smile. He was enjoying the dancers' efforts, as any red-blooded male would. Donna and Kelly were caressing each other, and soon they were kissing, lightly at first but then more deeply. As their excitement mounted, both girls lost their panties. Kelly pulled Donna's off first, and tossed them to David. He held them in his hand, rubbing the soft material between his fingers before lifting it to his face, and breathing in the subtle yet pungent scent of Donna's arousal. The chemical connections fired in his brain and his cock stretched out, demanding more room. He dropped his cigar into a stone pot, unzipped his trousers, and released his erection into the fire-lit chamber.

Kelly was now leaning forward into her husband's lap, anointing his cock with date wine and suckling his glans. She, too, had lost her panties, and Donna's face was buried deep between the cheeks of her bottom. The young blonde was enjoying a passionate rimming as her hips kept swaying to the music, taking Donna's head back and forth with them as her own face rose and fell over Rick's upright shaft.

It was a difficult position for Donna, squatting behind the other girl, and she eventually got up and moved to David. Their kiss was salty and dirty and much more intoxicating than the incense hanging in the air, replacing the sweet cloying smell with a much more potent scent. David pushed his fingers into the crotch of Donna's panties, and thrust it up between her sex lips. The material slipped easily between the slick folds of her labia, absorbing her wetness as he caressed her clitoris. Then he lifted the panties to his mouth, and sucked her fresh juices from the crotch.

She seemed to like that very much because she kissed him again passionately, and then stood before him caressing her breasts through the tight, boned bodice with one hand while running her other hand down her body and between her thighs. David enjoyed the show, especially the part where she turned around and reached down to grip her ankles. Her legs remained perfectly straight and slightly parted, giving him a good view of her deliciously available pussy.

Then, quite unexpectedly, she straightened up and walked across the room to a large statue of Osiris. His crossed arms held the symbols of State – a crook to tend his flock, and the multi-tailed whip of the flail with which to chastise them. She wrested the whip from the god's grasp, and turned to Kelly, who was still dutifully sucking her husband's cock. The blonde never saw or heard it coming, but she felt the sting of every single strip of leather as they kissed her bare bottom. She gasped from the sudden pain, and nearly gagged on the phallus rising up out of the throne from her husband's lap. He sat motionless as a god being worshipped, and closing her wide, startled eyes, she went passionately on with her oral devotions.

Rick smiled at Donna and drew on his cigar as he motioned for her to lay another stroke across his wife's pretty buttocks, and another, and another. Then, at a further signal from him, Donna grabbed a handful of Kelly's blonde hair and pulled her mouth off his erection.

'Time for the slave girl to be mounted,' she announced.

'Open your passage and let your master enter.'

Kelly dutifully opened her legs and inched herself over her husband's lap. Donna reached between her thighs, gripped Rick's cock, and positioned his helmet at the entrance to her friend's pussy with the sensual efficiency of a priestess performing an ancient rite.

Then Rick sat motionless on his throne and allowed his young slave wife to ride him with slow, tantalising movements of her slim hips. It was an erotic sight that made David want to sample the same treatment from Donna. He would have to wait, however, for Rick made another sign to Donna, which she interpreted and then translated for David.

'You are privileged,' she told him. 'Rickie wants you to mount Kelly.'

'I can't wait,' he replied enthusiastically, but Donna beckoned for him to approach the throne.

'You don't have to wait,' she went on. 'Rickie wants you to fuck her right now.'

David certainly enjoyed fucking young women up the arse, and liked to watch their expressions as they struggled to accommodate his cock in their tight sphincter. He glanced between Kelly's thighs, and saw the creamy lubricant of her juices glistening along the full length of Rick's erection as her pussy rode up and down. Above it, her stretched anus beckoned for more attention, and David quickly moved closer and edged forward between Rick's outstretched legs until he felt the warmth of Kelly's bottom touch his skin. Then Donna stepped up behind him, reached around his body, and gripped his penis.

'I'll put it in for you,' she said formally. 'You really are a very lucky man.'

David did not necessarily consider himself that fortunate.

After all, earlier in the day he had witnessed young Kelly's buttocks on the receiving end of a very impressive black cock. She was probably so stretched that he doubted she would even notice his presence. But apparently, he was not heading for the back door. Donna lowered his erection until his helmet touched the base of Rick's penis. This was new territory for David, in more ways than one, and his whole body tensed.

Feeling his reluctance, Donna gripped him more firmly. 'Open yourself up to new experiences,' she whispered. '*You* taught me that more than anyone.'

David allowed her to guide him closer to the unknown. He felt Kelly's stretched pussy slide down Rick's cock, and kiss his own solid rod. After several strokes the young woman stopped moving, and Donna used her fingers, as well as a guiding hand, to ease David's additional erection inside her friend. It was a struggle, and Kelly moaned and whimpered as the combined thickness of two hard cocks stretched her wide open, wider than she had ever been stretched before. The supple tightness of her hole expanded to its absolute limits before David managed to push past its resistance, and sink snugly up inside her on top of Rick's shaft. It was a strange sensation for all concerned, and it was a while before the two men realised the best effect was to be had when they thrust in unison.

'My, God,' Kelly gasped when they began fucking her in sync with each other, 'I'm so full… I'm so full…' She sounded a little frightened even as she added breathlessly, 'Oh, it feels so good…'

It was a great experience for the men as well as they derived much of their pleasure from her cries of ecstasy. David's enjoyment was further enhanced by the feel of Donna's tongue fervently licking his sphincter, and by the stimulating sensation of her finger penetrating him there.

To end with perfection, the men maintained eye contact so they knew when they were each close to coming and wanted to pick up the pace. Eventually they could contain themselves no longer. Forgetting the need to be gentle lest they hurt Kelly, and with coordination no longer possible as lust blinded them, they thrust and bucked inside her, and together released a torrent of sperm into her that triggered her own almighty release. She screamed, and the mingled pain and pleasure of her throbbing pussy unable to contract over two solid and swollen shafts as she climaxed nearly left her unconsciousness.

Donna gently pulled David's softening penis from Kelly, and led him back to his chair before helping Kelly down off Rick's lap and encouraging her to lie down on the stone floor. Then, as the men recovered with a drink, Donna knelt and dipped her head between the young woman's legs to enjoy a heady cocktail of come and cream.

Donna was the first to wake up in the shadowy Egyptian chamber. She crawled across the hard floor to David, who opened his eyes as her head began bobbing up and down the length of his cock, which was surprisingly hard again despite everything it had been through, and in. It was a wonderful way to wake up, and Rick appeared to have discovered another nice way. He was lying on top of his wife, riding her gently while squeezing her plump breasts between his fingers. No one spoke. They just sucked and fucked in silence, and then fell asleep once more.

When they all woke again, and finally emerged from the underground chamber, the house was dark. They had fucked away the entire evening.

'What time is it?' Donna asked, somewhat anxiously.

Kelly walked over to a large mantle clock, and peered into its face. 'It's almost eleven. You'd better telephone Doug and say you'll be staying over.'

Donna sighed. 'I can't,' she said. 'We're going to Denver tomorrow. Doug's got some business up there, and I said I'd go with him.'

'That's too bad.' Rick did not sound as if he cared, one way or the other. 'I felt like doing it all over again after we got something to eat.' He was obviously joking.

'Me too,' Kelly giggled. 'We still have time for a bath though, Donna. You can't go home looking like that.'

'I guess not,' Donna agreed.

Rick smiled, and pushed a button near the fireplace. A moment later a young Oriental woman entered into the room, and David abruptly realised there were servants living in the house. The girl wore black leather heels and a traditional black maid's dress. Rick ordered her to run a bath, and then to bring a tray of food and drinks up to the bathroom. The girl acknowledged his instructions with a polite bow, and departed without any indication that the sight of four naked people had surprised or upset her.

While Donna telephoned Doug to tell him she would be a little late getting home that night, Rick reset the snooker table. He closed one end, and the two slate slabs moved up to form the bed. Finally, the cloth was pulled across the table by silent motors and everything returned to normal.

The large bathroom was, not surprisingly, laid out like an ancient Roman spa, and in the centre of the marble tile floor was a walk-in tub large enough to have accommodated the entire senate.

The four of them enjoyed the hot water while talking about the latest movies. David had not seen any of them, but his companions seemed happy to fill him in on everything he had missed; he did not seem to have missed much, but he kept his opinions to himself.

The servant brought in some sliced fruit and a large pitcher of Sangria, and then she poured some oil in the water that filled the air with the relaxing scent of lavender. She left, and then returned again about half an hour later carrying four thick white towels and matching dressing gowns.

David sensed the evening was drawing to a close; Donna appeared increasingly anxious to get home, and Rick showed no signs of wanting to share Kelly again.

After everyone was dried off, and Donna and David were both dressed, goodnights were said. The men shook hands, the girls kissed each other on both cheeks, and then Donna guided David to the front door and escorted him back to his RV.

'It certainly was a surprise,' she said as they neared the carport, 'you turning up completely out of the blue like that.'

'I'm sorry I alarmed or upset you,' David apologised.

'You *did* alarm *and* upset me – for a moment or two,' Donna admitted.

'Because of what happened in Pakistan?'

'I thought you were a bastard for not helping me back there, you know that, don't you?'

'I told you, I was as scared as you were, Donna.'

'Yes, I realise that now, but I didn't at the time.' She fished her keys out of her purse, and then looked up into his eyes. 'But you know, in a way the experience made me stronger. It taught me how to look after myself.'

'It taught me that, too,' David acknowledged.

'So, we both gained something from it?'

'Yep, it certainly looks like it.'

She smiled, and held out her hand.

David took it, and then kissed her gently on the cheek. 'It was nice to see you again, Donna,' he said sincerely.

'It was nice to see you, too,' she echoed, turning away, 'as a free woman.'

Chapter Nine

Modesto was where David found himself when he woke up the next day. After leaving Rick Goldman's house, he spent a few hours driving and thinking. He had enjoyed a few crazy nights since Minnie went home to her mother, and yet he found he could not resist surfing the Net again in search of swingers, and sex.

He looked out over his campsite near Durham Ferry. Everything was green, and boring. He pulled open the cupboard above the sink, and reached for his shaving equipment. His reflection told him he looked as jaded as he felt. He had been drinking too much and smoking too much, and he had been having entirely too much sex. He was in need of a very good rest.

After his shave, he e-mailed Justin and told him he was beginning the cross-country leg of his journey. He expected to make it to Miami in about five or six days, and he asked his friend to book them a hotel there and then send the arrangements on to him.

It was still early in the morning. David had time to go for a stroll between the trees and commune with nature. He had intended all along to enjoy the excesses America had to offer, but he realised he was doing so at the expense of his spiritual side. Since his time in the Arctic, he had learned to love nature, and he had also discovered that nature tended to treat you more kindly if you respected it.

He walked for about an hour, and when he returned to the RV, he ate a large breakfast before taking a shower in the campsite washroom. His camper had a shower, but it lacked the space and power of the public facility.

By the time he took his place behind the wheel again, preparing for a twelve-hour drive to Las Vegas, he felt energised and refreshed, and with good music from his radio accompanying him on the journey, he set off for Yosemite.

Freed from his search for excitement and sexual pleasure, and half hypnotised by the long drive, David had lapsed into an almost dreamlike state by the time he reached and entered the national park. Without stopping to pick up any of the numerous backpackers taking the cheap route across country, he was making good time. He took a few hours getting through the park, and he even considered staying the night there because it reminded him so much of the Karelian peninsula, but he needed to keep to his schedule if he was going to make it to Miami in time to meet Justin, and so he pressed on.

As it happened, he had stayed inside the park longer than he realised, and exhaustion caught up with him before he reached Las Vegas. With the Funeral Mountains off in the distance, and Death Valley all around him, he decided to pull up and make camp.

The desert horizon wore the dying sun like a ruby ring as it set, sparkling with a last fiery, dazzling brilliance before plunging out of sight. Almost instantly, the temperature plummeted twenty degrees and night descended as if God had turned out the light.

Outside of a forest, and away from the city's concrete jungle, David felt quite vulnerable, and he experienced a twinge of anxiety. He had seen too many movies as a youngster to forget the hills had eyes. He was glad, therefore, to have found a rocky outcrop into which he could pull his RV off the road, and out of sight. This afforded him some peace of mind, at least.

Inevitably boredom set in, and he checked his e-mail. Justin had replied, and booked a hotel for them near the ocean. All the arrangements were made, and he was planning to fly out to see his old friend for a holiday. Before then, however, David had to decide if his vagabond days were over and if it was time to take root somewhere. Money, fortunately, was no object as he had become relatively wealthy during his travels.

He finished another beer, and then went to relieve himself in the desert, not wanting to use the toilet in the RV if it wasn't necessary. It was very cold outside, and he shivered as he stepped into the triangle of light cast by the open door of his vehicle. He walked a respectable distance, and urinated up against a large rock, allowing himself a smile at the thought that men always felt compelled to relieve themselves against something. For some base animal reason, the ground was never good enough.

He was putting his penis away when a faint flicker of light caught his attention. It was gone just as swiftly, and for a moment he waited to hear the engine of a car passing on the road. The desert remained silent, however, and he felt a touch of fear when he saw a light flicker again. The beam was being reflected off some rocks leading into a gully.

He knew he shouldn't, but like a moth drawn to a flame he found himself creeping towards the source of the illumination, and in the darkness of the desert, with no real landmarks to guide him, he misjudged the distance. The light was a lot further than he had realised, but it was growing brighter, and then he heard voices.

They stopped him in his tracks, and he spent a few

moments thinking about his next move hoping the loud thumping of his heart would not give him away. There were people in the gully and, as he composed himself, he realised curiosity was one aspect of his character he could not control. But he was not stupid enough to blunder into the scene like some absentminded hiker, and so he sought another way to try and discern the source of the light.

It was a ten-minute climb, and the outcome was a frightening revelation. A few hundred feet below him, and about fifty feet further away, blazed a fire around which sat two bikers. Next to one of them a naked girl crouched on her hands and knees, her head near the ground, her bottom thrust up into the air. The light of the fire played across her buttocks, and revealed that the biker beside her was using her arsehole as a receptacle for his cigarette.

A third biker was busy fucking another girl spread-eagled across the sand, her wrists and ankles attached to wooden pegs driven into the ground. The two unoccupied men were talking and drinking. David could not make out what they were saying, but during a lull in the conversation the biker next to the crouching girl pulled the cigarette from her arse, and began smoking it again. His companion then leaned back on his arms, and casually kicked her as he said something. She fell across the sand, but then quickly picked herself up and ran towards one of the tents. She disappeared inside it for a moment, and emerged holding a six-pack of beer. She handed it to the biker who had been using her anus as a cigarette holder, and he promptly pulled her down to her knees and shoved her face down into his lap.

The other man watched the girl sucking his friend's cock for a moment before he rose unsteadily to his feet, and made his way to the couple on the sand. He kicked the man, and his gesture made it clear he was impatiently waiting his turn. Some angry words were exchanged, but the man on his feet apparently possessed seniority, because the other biker climbed reluctantly off the girl.

She too, was naked, and looked quite relaxed lying across the sand with her legs spread wide open. David did not doubt she belonged to one, or maybe all, of the bikers. And it was then he realised he recognised the first girl, the one beside the fire. It was Angel, the slut from Gang Bang Ranch. And when he crept nearer to confirm his suspicions, the scar cutting the seated biker's face in half left no doubt as to his identity. It was Jake.

For a wild moment David panicked and believed they were following him. He nearly stood up and ran back to the RV so he could put some distance between them, but he fought the desire to flee and managed to compose himself. He lay flat on his belly and rested his chin on his knuckles as he continued looking down at the scene.

Why would they be after him? Maybe because he stole their prize when they were all sleeping, and humiliated them? But they never saw him. How would they know he did it? And yet how could he be sure no one saw him? A truck driver back at the diner might have seen him return with Minnie, and put two and two together... But how would they know he came this way? There again, and more to the point, did he care how they knew? The fact was, they were there.

He tore his eyes away from the partying bikers, and turned over onto his back. There was not a single cloud in the star-filled sky. If only his head was as clear. He turned back in time to see Bobby suddenly stand up, and point to something just out of David's line of sight. The biker marched straight towards it as Jake immediately pushed Angel off his lap, got up, and followed the younger man out of sight.

David held his breath in nervous anticipation.

A moment later they reappeared, and Bobby was carrying something that obviously excited him. He stabbed the object with a long screwdriver he pulled from his boot, and held it over the fire. David could not be absolutely sure, but he suspected the biker had found a peyote cactus. He smiled to himself. This meant he was safe for the night. If they ate the peyote before it was fully dried out, which they obviously planned to do, the mescaline would give them a very intense trip indeed. Native American shamans valued peyote for its hallucinogenic properties, and the white man was certainly not beyond appreciating its mind-bending capabilities.

Before David sneaked back to his RV, and a good night's sleep, he noticed that the third unknown biker was the only one who did not partake of the magical cactus.

David did not order fried green tomatoes at the *Whistle Stop Café*, though he had no doubt that many people did, thanks to the movie. For breakfast, he made do with ham and eggs and a glass of orange juice while reading the numerous flyers sorted into piles on the tables. Each one was a free ticket to varying shows and events in Las Vegas.

He was idly reading a blurb when the door of the restaurant opened, and two leather-clad men entered with two scantily clad girls in tow. They looked in need of a meal, of a wash, and of the address of a tailor, not necessarily in that order. David's heart missed a beat, and his passing interest in the delights of the *Flamingo Gaming Room* developed into a passion as he bowed his head intently over the flyer, his eyes reading and re-reading the same line without his brain absorbing the words.

The bikers behaved themselves, however. They collected some food in a civilised fashion and then, as bad luck would have it, chose the table next to David's, where the waitress caught up with them and brought them some coffee. The small gang looked drained by their psychedelic night out in the desert.

'More coffee, mister?'

It was not the waitress's voice that attracted the bikers' attention, it was David's sudden, guilty voice nearly shouting, 'Oh yes, please.'

Bobby recognised him immediately. 'Hey, you're the dude from Coos Bay, I remember you.'

David feigned ignorance while thinking fast. He realised they were not following him after all, which meant they probably had no suspicions that it was he who had spirited Minnie away as they slept.

Yet despite his relief, he thought it wise to say as little as possible, and to get away from the *Whistle Stop Café* at the earliest opportunity. Which was not to come soon, he realised, as the group suddenly picked up their plates and their coffees, and came and joined him at his table as if he was their oldest and dearest friend.

'You must remember us,' Bobby pressed him. 'In the roadhouse, near the Bay, you had some sexy little hiker bitch with you, and you left her with us.'

'Oh yes, I remember,' he said without conviction.

Bobby laughed. 'Listen to that accent. It's great, isn't it? You were cool, man, not nervous at all about playing pool with a bunch of bikers. Well, you might like to know that lovely babe you left with us pulled the longest train ever to run down the West coast. She was at it all night.'

'Not all night, surely,' David said, chancing a bit of fun.

'I'm telling you, we kept her at it all fucking night, man.

When the guys weren't riding her, Angel here was buttering her pussy.'

David looked at the wild-haired girl, and smiled remembering her with Minnie.

'We owe you one,' Bobby added. 'Do you like playing cards?'

'We can't, Bobby.' Jake scowled. 'The *man* wouldn't like it.'

'Who's asking him?' Bobby retorted.

Even Jake suddenly looked nervous. 'Listen, get your English friend pissed some other time, we got business to attend to here.'

'Look, I told you, we owe him one,' Bobby insisted. 'Besides, he can handle himself. I know he can.'

The others resigned themselves to the fact that the Englishman was invited, and Bobby asked David if he had heard of *Gambelli's*.

'It's a small-time gambling joint,' he explained, 'two blocks from the strip, between the armoury and the Elvis wedding chapel.'

As he made a mental note of the directions, David noticed the third biker standing outside. He was using the public phone and staring into the café. Both his leather vest and his jeans looked strangely clean, almost new.

They entered the town in a cavalcade. Jake and Bobby rode up front with the girls, David formed the middle in his RV, and the unknown biker made up the rear. There was no turning off the road for David and trying to lose them, not unless he wanted to make enemies, and there was a lot of desert out there – plenty of places to run, but nowhere to hide.

The gaudy neon signs and the multitude of flashing

coloured lights David associated with Las Vegas were nowhere to be seen. *Gambelli's* looked like some drinking hole straight out of a spaghetti western, and they even had to cross a dirt road to get to it. He was happy with the rather downbeat feel of the place; the high-tech, corporate image of the major casinos was much too clinical for his tastes.

The group stepped inside, and again David was pleasantly surprised. The bar could very well have been a saloon in the old Wild West. Painted mirrors touting the virtues of bourbon and tobacco formed the backdrop of a long, liquor-stained bar. There were a few hand-pumps for dispensing beer, but spirits were clearly the beverages of choice for the locals. Tourists did not appear to be welcome, for there were none in evidence, as far as David could tell.

'Can I help you?' The Mexican barman, his bald scalp as polished as his antique mirrors, showed no signs of apprehension faced with three dangerous looking bikers. Behind him, David saw the baseball bat he guessed contributed to the man's confidence. Two bullet holes in the bar also suggested the bat had other, more persuasive friends to call upon, if necessary.

Bobby ordered bourbon for every one.

'I'll have a beer,' David said, 'it's more refreshing in this heat.'

He was the last to be served, and while the bartender waited for the head on his beer to recede, the others downed their shots.

Then the Mexican did what David had been hoping he would do – he slammed the glass down on the bar, and slid it straight to him. David caught it, lifted it, and swallowed long and often. It was a priceless moment.

'Good beer,' he said with a broad smile. 'So, Bobby,

what brings you south?'

'Fun, and business,' the biker replied. 'Let's sit down.'

A table by the window easily accommodated six people. As he grabbed a chair, David noticed a black Cadillac parked across the road, and two men sitting inside it. He was about to point them out when Jake asked him what he was doing in the United States.

'Oh, you know, enjoying the sights and wondering if I should stay,' David replied breezily.

'It's the only place to be,' Jake stated in a tone that dared anyone to contradict him. 'No place better on God's green earth.'

David thought it a strange comment for such an aggressive man to make, and raised his glass in a toast-like fashion. 'To the land of opportunity,' he declared. 'If you can't make money in America, you must be stupid.'

'Or dead.'

It was the first words David had heard the unknown biker speak, and everyone found them quite funny, except him. Nevertheless, he smiled politely even as he kept his eyes on the Cadillac parked across the street.

Bobby called for another round of drinks, and the bartender brought them over. Then Angel pulled a pack of cigarettes from her pocket, and everyone decided to follow her example. 'When are we going into town, Bobby?' she asked plaintively. 'I want some fun.'

'Yeah,' the other girl piped in. 'I thought you said we'd be hitting the casinos.'

'Soon, baby,' Bobby assured one, or both of them with this blanket endearment.

David noticed a certain tension had crept into his voice, and that he kept glancing at the clock behind the bar.

'Hey,' Bobby suddenly looked at David, 'you want to

come with us later when we hit the casinos?'

'I never win,' David said, by way of declining the offer.

'You'll win this time, I guarantee it.'

'Hello, Bobby.'

No one had heard the three men enter. David looked outside. The Cadillac was gone.

'Hitting the bottle a little early, aren't you, Bobby?'

'Been a long drive, Dino,' Bobby said. 'Just wetting our throats. Wanna join us?'

Dino looked around, and so did his two companions. 'Let's find another table,' he said. He was a tall, well-dressed, rather handsome dark-haired man, like his friends.

David felt himself grow suddenly tense. He was caught up in something – something that made him very uneasy – and he could not think of any way to extricate himself now.

But Dino was about to give him one. 'Rico,' he called to the bartender, 'any rooms free so we can get a card game going?'

Rico nodded, and pointed to a side door.

'After you, gentlemen,' Dino said. His companions had spoken not a word, until one of them abruptly focused on David.

'Who's he?' the man asked sharply.

'Just a friend, we owed a drink,' Bobby replied. 'You should have seen the bitch he—'

'Are you crazy?' Dino demanded between clenched teeth. 'Do you even know who the fuck he is?'

'I told you,' Bobby stayed cool, 'he's just some English guy on holiday who dropped a pretty little hiker off for us a few days ago.' He turned to David. 'Say something, man.'

David's throat seemed to dry up, but he finally managed to mutter, 'Hello, pleasure to meet you all.'

'He comes in with us,' Dino said firmly.

'Why?' Jake demanded.

The atmosphere was becoming decidedly charged.

'He's coming with us,' Dino repeated.

David ended up following everyone to the back room. Unlike the rest of the bar, the room was modern, with boring white plastered walls and nothing in the way of decor. It was dominated by a large round table surrounded by chairs, and the only natural light had to sneak in through two high and very narrow windows.

Everyone sat down except David, the girls, and the mysterious biker. The latter remained by the door, and David made himself comfortable against the wall trying to suppress a sense of foreboding.

Bobby produced a bottle of bourbon, and one of the men in suits spread a number of shot glasses across the table. The seated men took a drink, and then Bobby handed one to David.

'How much?' Dino asked, setting his briefcase on the table.

Bobby smiled, and looked at Jake before replying, 'Two hundred.'

It was Dino's turn to smile. 'That's a lot of money. Business must be good.'

'That depends on what your man's giving.'

Dino opened his case, and David noticed a handgun lying across some gold casino checks, but all Dino pulled out was a calculator. He pressed a few keys. 'He says seventy cents to the dollar.'

'You don't need a fucking adding machine for that, man,' Bobby snapped, 'it's a hundred and forty grand, and that's shit. We can get more across the border.'

Dino's smile deepened dangerously. 'I'm just telling you

what the boss said.'

'We want *eighty* cents,' Jake practically spit the words out. 'So you can tell the man, no fucking deal.'

David downed his drink, and held his breath.

Dino held his hand up as his colleagues watched him carefully. 'I've got some influence with the man.' He spoke with quiet confidence. 'I think I can vouch for him on this matter and offer you seventy-five cents. I'll smooth it out with him later.'

'*Fuck* him,' Jake shouted. 'I say we go to the Mexicans.'

Bobby looked at the nameless biker. 'What do you say?'

David was very relieved to hear the man reply, no matter how curt his response. 'Take it. We've got a deal here. It'll waste time setting up another meeting. I say we take seventy-five. If the Mexicans offer us less, then what do we do, come crawling back here for fifty?'

Bobby nodded. 'The man always stands by his word. We'll take seventy-five.'

Dino's smile appeared to be painted on as he collected the gold checks from his briefcase. 'The usual deal,' he said. 'Present these checks at the tables and you'll walk away with a hundred and fifty grand. You get clean money, and we make a little profit in exchange for washing your notes.'

Jake downed a shot of bourbon. 'Yeah, but we take all the chances.'

'Seems like a good deal to me,' Dino replied smoothly. 'Now, where's the cash?'

'It's in the tank of a chopper outside,' Bobby told him.

Dino looked impressed. 'You take chances.'

Bobby laughed. 'Who's going to steal a biker's hog? Some fucker with a death wish?'

For the briefest of moments the tension lifted, but the

peace was short-lived. With a loud crashing sound the door to the room suddenly burst open as someone kicked it in.

'Hands up!' a man yelled. 'Hands up where I can fucking see them!'

David felt his stomach convulse as he recognised the two men from the Cadillac. He held himself perfectly still, and said a silent prayer.

Dino's smile thinned to the point where it looked more like a grimace. 'We'll find you,' he warned quietly. 'This country's not big enough for you to hide in. Someone will talk.'

'Shut the fuck up!' the man holding the gun barked, unaware of the fact that the nameless biker, who had been standing behind the door when it was kicked open, was now holding a sawn-off shotgun to the back of his head.

'You're too fucking early,' the clean-cut biker said furiously, 'the fucking money's not here yet.'

'Blow the bastard away,' Jake growled, nodding towards the second gunman. 'They can't shoot us all.'

It seemed to David that control was about to switch away from the men at the door to the table, but he was very wrong, for the nameless biker abruptly trained his shotgun on the group he had ridden into town with.

'The money's in Bobby's chopper outside,' he said calmly.

Jake made to get up, but stopped himself. 'I knew there was something fucking rotten about you,' he hissed. 'I just fucking knew it!'

'You want to see my badge? Go and get the money,' he said to the second man from the Cadillac, 'we'll clean up here. It's the bike with the green tank.'

David looked back at Dino. His hand was inside his briefcase.

192

Who fired the first shot was a matter for the Las Vegas PD to determine. It seemed to David that the room had suddenly exploded with gunfire. Smoke burned his eyes and his brain shut down in response to the ear-splitting reports. The shooting could not have gone on for more than two or three seconds, yet it felt like an eternity. He had no way of knowing how long it lasted, all he knew was that he was still breathing, and wasn't aware of any life-threatening pains anywhere on his body. His only injury turned out to be a bump on the forehead he got diving for cover under the table.

After the riot of gunfire ceased, an eerie silence descended over the room. David did not even think of calling for help, as he knew none would be forthcoming.

'I knew you were cool…' Bobby's voice was barely a whisper.

'I'll get some help,' David said.

'No point.' The biker lifted his hand to reveal a hole the size of a fist in his belly. 'It's your lucky day,' he groaned. His face was a mask of pain as he reached into his denim pocket, and pulled out the key to his bike. 'Take it,' he urged.

David took the key, there was no point arguing with a dying man. Then he quickly got to his feet and made for the door, too squeamish to check on the state of anyone else's health. The floor was strewn with bodies, and their stillness, not to mention the pools of blood spreading around them, did not bode well.

The first hungry flies had just begun entering the room when David closed the door behind him.

There was a decision to be made, and not much time in which to make it. Remarkably, David felt calm as he stepped outside into the blazing sunshine. He did not hear any police sirens in the distance, and the street looked just as it had before. He walked over to the bikes, kicked up the stand on the bike with the green tank, and pushed it across to his RV. A minute later he had attached the chopper to the rear bike mounts and was pulling slowly away from *Gambelli's*.

He drove five hundred miles before he stopped again.

It was all there, all two hundred thousand dollars, crammed inside a false cover sitting over the original tank. It took David over an hour to count the money.

His problem now was what to do with the bike. If he dumped it at the side of the road out in the middle of nowhere, there was a chance it would be reported to the police. The same thing would happen if he attempted to burn it. The best thing to do was to head for Albuquerque and leave the bike parked on the street. That way, it might just sit there for a day or two before someone reported it. More likely than not, it would be stolen, and then it would either be cut down or repainted and driven until it fell apart. Whatever happened, abandoning it on a street somewhere would put time and distance between him and the hot vehicle.

The day after he left the bike outside a bar in Albuquerque, David woke up to a beautiful morning near a tiny settlement called Nogal on the road to Roswell and the infamous air force base. He had spent a fitful night waiting for the sound of police sirens that, fortunately, never materialised. The bloody event had not even made the six o'clock news. Finally, he found a brief report on a local Internet news site that put the violence down to a dispute between members of the Las Vegas underworld and a group of bikers from out of town. The police issued a statement that they were not looking for any suspects because a large amount of valuable casino checks had been found at the scene. The motive had clearly been robbery, and since the checks were still there it meant the potential thief had been killed along with everyone else. David looked to be in the clear.

He ate some breakfast, and then checked his e-mail. He had a few messages from some Frisco Swingers he could do nothing about now, and a nice note from Donna thanking him for a good time, and wishing him a safe journey. He laughed out loud.

The last message was from Justin. He was flying to Miami in two days' time. If David drove for two days and two nights with only brief stops, he could make it there in time to meet his friend, but he decided on a compromise. He would drive to New Orleans, and from there fly to Miami. He e-mailed Justin his plans, and took his familiar position in the driver's seat.

'Excuse me,' a girl's voice said through his open window. 'Are you going to Roswell? I sure would appreciate a lift.'

David saw long blonde hair blowing across a young woman's pretty features. 'Jump in,' he said. 'That's just where I'm headed.'

Chapter Ten

It was a shame for David to be making the last leg of his journey more of a race than a tour, but he had agreed to meet Justin in Miami so they could look for a nice property in sunny Florida together. David doubted this was going to be possible now. Sooner or later the police would find out about the Englishman who suddenly disappeared from *Gambelli's* after the shootout. They would come looking for him, and he had learned, to his cost, that a man could even be found in the icy wastes of Siberia. He wanted to spend a day or two enjoying the Florida sun, but then it was almost certain he would have to leave America and keep travelling.

He had about a day-and-a-half to make it to Shreveport and from there to New Orleans. For the moment, he was enjoying some iced tea and pancakes while commerce clattered its noisy way along the interstate.

He squinted against the nearly blinding sunlight, closed his eyes, and drifted back to Roswell and Cindy, the hiker. God, he loved girls named Cindy, and there were so many of them, blonde-haired, blue-eyed and pert-breasted, hitchhiking and carrying their fares inside well-stacked T-shirts. This particular Cindy was no different. She was pretty, she was American, and she was looking for new experiences. That's why she wanted to see Roswell.

'It's a cover-up!' she told him in an excited whisper. 'The military picked up the bodies of some aliens there years ago.'

The experiences she got were not the ones she was searching for, but David liked to think they were more enlightening than the pointless pursuit of lost aliens. He showed her that the real danger lies not in the interior of a spaceship from another galaxy, but in the interior of a Chevy, a Pontiac, a Nissan, or even a family camper driven by a polite Englishman.

He was not usually a cruel man, but he had been strangely energised by the long journey – by his experiences on the road with Minnie, by meeting up with Donna again, by barely escaping a violent death and, of course, by picking up two hundred thousand dollars along the way.

Naturally, Cindy was not averse to a little sexual play. That was the hitchhiker's standard fare and she did not mind paying. She was, after all, an active young woman, and she did not even baulk at a little light bondage; she found it thrilling. She was a little more nervous about the blindfold and the gag, but even they seemed to heighten her excitement, and David's sophisticated accent reassured her. What he was saying also added a certain amount of frisson to her sexual tension. He was telling her how completely helpless she was, and that he could do anything he wanted to her. The threat scared her, but no more than it turned her on.

The feel of his leather belt on her bare bottom was the first indication that the mixture was a bit too rich for her. The light lashes gradually increasing in intensity, and the calm voice commanding her to hold still, soon became quite frightening to her. With a ball gag in her mouth, she had no way of protesting against the pain, no way of indicating her displeasure, no way of pleading for him to stop. The whipping went on, and on. At first he only beat her bottom, but then he moved up to her back, and finally he could not resist turning her around and giving her a few exceedingly cruel strokes across her breasts.

When he knew she felt as though her whole body was on fire, he finally stopped. She was totally at his mercy, and she moved her body compliantly in whatever direction he desired, which happened to be face down over the table again, her cheek pressed against the cold Formica surface and her arms lashed firmly behind her.

She pushed her bottom back towards him, offering him both entrances into her body. David did not rush, smiling at the thought that she undoubtedly expected a rectal probe now since an Englishman was technically considered an alien in the United States. Then he remembered Minnie's experiences with rum, and searched the cupboard. He found a bottle of vodka, and trickled a little into the sweet hollow of her back. The liquid felt cool at first, but then its high alcohol content started to burn and she squirmed against the table, moaning through her ball gag. David chose this highly inviting moment to thrust his impatient cock into her pussy. She writhed even more violently at his sudden invasion, and her clenched vagina formed the perfect sheathe for his iron-hard rod. When she looked as though she was beginning to relax and enjoy his deep strokes, he spanked her hard a few times, adding more pain to her pleasure.

It was not long before the drawn out combination of fear and excitement, torment and ecstasy, led to the unmistakable signs of an orgasm tearing through her flesh. It was a terrifyingly powerful experience for Cindy. Her body screamed for release, but her bonds held fast, so when a climax suddenly found a way through, and freed her, her whole body stiffened in disbelief at the intensity of the pleasure.

David kept right on fucking her after she came, with the goal of making her clitoris supersensitive, while promising her that when he was finished with her pussy he was going to fuck her arse. But then he decided he preferred to sample both her holes at once. So as she squealed into her gag he penetrated her bottom, enjoyed its delicious tightness for a few moments, and then returned to her slick pussy. He kept this up for a long time, sometimes pulling out of whatever orifice he was enjoying, and then thrusting right back in just to shock her, because she had expected him to switch. Everything he did was designed to increase her confusion and her torment and, inevitably, her pleasure.

The hours passed, and she became increasingly weak from all the attention he was paying her. Then at last David decided it was time for him to have mercy on her, and ejaculated deep inside her bottom. Her body went limp beneath the sensation of his eruption, and she moaned at this final, humiliating caress.

David sipped his iced tea and smiled in satisfaction. Cindy had proved very satisfying. She had also surprised him. Once she realised she was not in any danger with him, she began talking about the intensity of her feelings when she was helpless. He listened, and then enjoyed her body again, both inside and outside the RV, where he chased her naked across the desert and played out her abduction fantasy by dragging her back into his vehicle, and subjecting her to another thorough examination of her anus with his rigid penis. She admitted to harbouring violent fantasies ever since she took to the road and a truck driver made her suck his cock in return for a lift. She had been hitching rides ever since, always hoping to go one further, always looking for the next experience.

David dropped her off at Roswell, and gave her three thousand dollars to keep her off the road for a while. He knew it wouldn't.

He arrived in New Orleans late in the evening and decided to stay in a hotel for the night. He booked a room in *The Lafayette*, and then walked to a restaurant where he ate Cajun chicken watching the rain bouncing off the pavement and turning to steam in the oppressive heat. As quickly as the downpour began, it ceased, and the only evidence of its brief appearance were the colourful serpents of reflected neon light slithering in the oily kerbside water.

New Orleans had its own definite smell – the pervasive harbour scent of salt water and fish mixed with a hint of spice, and the heavy sensual essence of sweat-borne pheromones emanating from every tobacco-filled Creole bar.

A black waitress with flawless skin, her hair pulled tightly back away from the beautiful bones of her face, lit David's cheroot for him before taking his empty plate away. He watched her tight bottom saunter away, and called after her. When she turned back towards him, he once again admired her features and asked for another bottle of red wine. The girl recognised his interest in her – it was not unexpected or unique – which was why she was irritated by his lack of response when she brought him the bottle he had requested, and then remained hovering at his elbow. She was awaiting further instructions, or at least a hint of appreciation, but none were forthcoming. She followed David's gaze to a restaurant across the street. The new object of his attention was a blonde woman sitting framed by a French door closed against the wet weather. Her white skirt and jacket looked expensive, and her stockinged feet sat snugly inside white shoes with stiletto heels. The waitress smirked, and left him alone with his bottle and his blonde.

Through the humid atmosphere, and in the glow from an oil lamp on the table beside her, David saw a softly focused vision of serene beauty. She was not alone. Her two companions were a glass of what looked like whisky, and a very tall, equally well-dressed, black man. He was not actually with her, however; he stood to one side of her table. David smoked his cheroot and drank his wine and watched the blonde pull a silver case from her white handbag. She held a cigarette up to her red lips, and the big black man promptly leaned forward and lit it for her. She did not acknowledge his action. She simply smoked silently, lost in her own thoughts. David could have watched her all night, but his bladder was demanding attention. He held out for ten more minutes, and then finally got up and went in search of the toilets.

When he emerged his heart missed a beat. The beautiful blonde was there, in his restaurant, and she was actually sitting at his table, the tip of a fresh cigarette embraced by her crimson lips, her silky legs crossed. And beside her towered the black man who seemed to be her shadow. For a moment David hesitated, trying to think, but he did precious little of that before arriving at his own table feeling like the interloper.

'I saw you watching me,' she explained at once. She looked to be in her late twenties, but she had the deep, smoky voice of a much older and more experienced woman. 'You intrigued me, so I thought I would introduce myself.'

'Right,' David replied, rather stupidly. 'May I?'

'It's your table,' she reminded him soberly. 'I hope you don't think I'm being rude.'

'Not at all,' he assured her. He sat down gingerly, keeping his eye on the black man, who had yet to speak. 'I've only just arrived in the city,' he added.

As she stubbed out her cigarette, he noticed that her fingernails matched her bold red lipstick. 'I'm Monique Petain.' She held her hand out formally. 'You're English?'

'Yes, though I haven't been to England for a while.'

'Oh?' She pulled out another cigarette, and the black man lit it for her right on cue. 'There is a reason for that?' She blew the smoke over David's head.

'Just travelling,' he replied, strangely at a loss for words. 'Seeking new experiences.'

'That's interesting... I'm sorry, I didn't catch your name.'

'David.'

'Maybe I could show you something of old Louisiana, David. Would you like that?' She gave him the faintest of smiles while holding him in her cool blue eyes.

'That would be lovely,' he said, 'but I'm afraid I'll be leaving tomorrow. I'm flying to Miami.'

'Then let me show you tonight,' she insisted. 'I see you've already eaten. What were you planning to do now, go to bed early?'

'N-no,' he stammered. 'Where were you thinking of taking me?'

'To my plantation.' With an elegant tilt of her head, she indicated the tall black man standing behind her chair. 'Jubal will drive us.'

She owned a Range Rover, which naturally, was air-conditioned. It was not soundproof, however, and as they travelled south out of the city, every time it came to a stop at an intersection it sounded as if millions of crickets and frogs and other unknown swamp dwellers were surrounding the vehicle. Nature seemed prepared to encroach upon technology once and for all in the Louisiana swamps.

After some time they passed an airfield.

'Oh yes,' she said almost absentmindedly. 'I think I can solve your flight problem tomorrow, David.'

'It's not really a problem,' he said warily. 'I just need to book a ticket.'

'Well, anyway, I shall fly you there myself. I haven't flown in over a month. I could use the practice.' She smiled at him.

'You're a pilot?' he declared rather foolishly, but this woman was so beautiful and so sure of herself, she made him feel as nervous as a boy.

'It would be silly of me to pretend I could fly if I couldn't, don't you think?'

'Sorry, I didn't mean to imply… I mean, I was just surprised.'

'Would you like a cigarette?' she asked, dismissing the subject.

The car sped on for several more miles, and each one took them deeper into the swamp. Sometimes the road disappeared beneath a blanket of mist, and Jubal seemed to make his way by pure instinct between increasingly large and almost grotesquely twisted trees, their decrepit limbs draped in moss. The darkness became almost oppressive, and David felt a profound sense of foreboding possessing him.

But it lifted somewhat when the car turned onto a paved driveway and he saw a huge white mansion looming against the black sky. The drive was illuminated by a row of torches leading up to the large double doors, and the place had French colonial stamped all over it, as did the young black girl with her hair tied in colourful bunches of rags who ran out to meet the car. She opened the back door, and welcomed her mistress home.

'Light the fire in the sitting room, Maisey,' Monique instructed her. 'As you can see, I have a guest.'

The girl rushed off, but then abruptly turned and ran back. 'M-madam,' she stammered.

'Yes, what is it, Maisey?'

'There's been some trouble in the village, madam.'

'What kind of trouble?'

The girl seemed unsure of how to answer that, but eventually she blurted that Leena had been caught in someone else's bed, someone other than her husband's, that is. The offended spouse was understandably put out by the matter, and demanding that the rules of the house be enforced. The others, whoever the others were, had not succeeded in calming him down.

By now, Jubal had walked around the car and was standing beside his mistress.

'Go and see to it Jubal,' she said a little wearily, and then turned back to Maisey. 'Go light a fire in the sitting room,' she repeated patiently.

Maisey turned on her heels again, and this time ran all the way into the house.

Jubal walked purposefully towards the side of the mansion as David followed Monique up to the front doors. They opened onto a large hall in which the right wall consisted of a row of tall glass doors covered by transparent white curtains. David discovered that they opened onto a magnificent sight – the Gulf of Mexico, its warm waves washing the shore of the plantation just a few hundred yards away. The twinkling lights of boats could be seen undulating on the water, but even more incredible were the lights burning inside dozens of wooden huts dotting the lawn of the great house. The whole scene appeared to be painted on a grey-blue canvas in the impressionist style, and occasionally a firefly flickered close to the veranda before vanishing again in its haunting search for a mate in the darkness.

'The village?' David asked quietly, feeling as though he had been transported back into another time.

'Yes, for my workers.' Monique walked across to another door, and opened it. 'Would you like a drink?'

He followed her into the room just as Maisey was leaving it. The girl had lit a large fire, and a few romantic gas lamps, by whose combined light David could see that the room was decorated in a colonial style perfectly in keeping with the architecture of the house. Two armchairs sat on either side of the dancing flames, and Monique handed him a glass of red wine before choosing her seat.

'This is a beautiful house,' he told her. In his mind's eye, he was trying to figure out how she could afford it. She had not mentioned a husband and she did not look old enough to have amassed a fortune big enough to pay for it. He imagined she must have inherited her money, either from her father or from a late spouse.

'It's the oldest working plantation in Louisiana, and we've owned it since my family came from France generations ago,' she informed him as if reading his mind. 'I told you I would show you something of the old world.'

'It's incredible. I thought this way of life had vanished long ago.'

Monique collected a cigarette from another silver case sitting on a small side table. 'It did,' she replied blithely, 'everywhere except here, where almost everything is still done the old way. We hand pick our cotton and make our own cloth. There's a premium for such quality material.'

'But the people in the village, I would have thought they'd

have left in search of a better life.'

'They did leave, before my grandfather's time. But what was there to do?' She shrugged her delicate shoulders. 'Families wandered the swamps trying to make a living, and a lot of them starved. Many came back. The old life was harsh, but it was secure. A home, food, a purpose.'

'But what keeps them here now?'

She crossed her legs and blew smoke up towards an unlit chandelier. 'The same things, I imagine. They can leave if they want to and face the modern world. I can't force them to stay.' She got up abruptly, and motioned for David to join her by the window. 'You see those groups of huts over there? That's the retirement village. When they can no longer work in the fields, they have a guaranteed house here. How much would that cost in the big city?'

David had no idea, and so simply shook his head.

'A lot of money,' she assured him. 'They would need very good jobs outside to afford a retirement like this, right on the ocean surrounded by their loved ones, not locked up in some horrible nursing home. So they stay and work for me.'

They were returning to their seats when there was a knock at another door leading into the room. Monique called for the person to enter, and a man who looked to be in his late thirties walked in.

'What is it, George?'

'Please, madam,' he began respectfully, 'you gave Leena to me, and now she's lying down with that young buck.' Apparently, he could not bring himself to say the other man's name.

'I gave her to you, George, because you have no children. I was hoping Leena would be expecting a child by now, but she's not, so I'm not surprised she should seek another man's bed.'

George looked embarrassed, and his gaze dropped to the carpet. 'But we have rules, madam,' he reminded her. 'If they're not kept, the village will be lawless.'

'I bent those rules for you, George. You know that. If a man fails to make his new wife pregnant within a year, then she's put to Jubal, and Jubal will stud her until a child is sired. That's the rule. Yet you begged me not to put her to Jubal. If I bring Leena in now for her punishment, then you must accept the other condition.'

George literally wrung his hands in despair. Jubal had many children running around the village. Many men had seen their wives taken away until Jubal planted his seed inside her and made her conceive. However, once she was pregnant she returned to her husband. Considering all this, George finally nodded his agreement.

'Where is Leena now?' Monique asked him.

'Outside,' he replied.

'Then send her in, and bring Jubal here as well. We shall kill two birds with one stone.'

George knew what that meant, and so did David, who thought it was a particularly cruel twist to send the husband to fetch the man about to mount his wife.

A few minutes after George left, three women escorted a struggling Leena into the fire-lit room. At first David could not get a good look at the girl because she was twisting so violently in the arms of her escorts, but Monique brought her under control simply by saying her name. Leena immediately became passive, and the women released her.

Monique turned to David and motioned for him to stand up. 'Clear the hearth,' she instructed the women, who promptly began moving the chairs away and taking everything off the mantelpiece. When they had finished,

Monique faced Leena.

'Why do you lie down with another man when I have given you to George?' she asked directly.

'I did not want George,' Leena replied, holding her mistress's eyes. 'He is a good man but he is old, so I went to Gilly for comfort.'

David could understand that. Leena looked to be no more than eighteen-years-old, and although her billowing skirt and blouse did little for her figure, her face was exquisitely beautiful.

'Does George not satisfy you?' Monique demanded. 'Does he not perform his duties?'

'Not like a man who wants to possess me, he has no passion. He mounts me and rides me like a man without a heart. No children can be made when there is no fire in the man's thighs.'

The door behind Leena opened, and in stepped Jubal, followed by George. Leena turned her head, and her eyes widened when she saw the whip in Jubal's hand. She looked back at her mistress and sank to her knees. 'Please, madam, do not whip me,' she begged passionately.

But her plea fell on deaf ears. Monique stepped aside, and the women took that as their signal to grab Leena's wrists and drag her over to the fireplace, holding her centred between them. For a moment David feared Leena's skirt would touch the flames, but a large matronly woman yanked it down, forcing Leena to step out of it. Her blouse was also then stripped off her, and now the young black woman was completely naked. Her skin was so smooth and lustrous it shone like a wet hazelnut caressed by the firelight. She also had the smallest, firmest bottom David had ever seen.

Jubal stepped forward, took up his position slightly to Leena's left, and shook the whip out. It was short, resembling a supple cane with a switch connected to the end. The big black man loosened his wrist, Monique gave him the signal, and he slashed the strip of leather across the young woman's back with a loud crack that resounded across the room. David expected a scream to follow, but the girl was silent. He looked at her back, and saw evidence of the cruel power of the blow smiling garishly from her shoulder all the way down to her bottom.

Leena did not make a sound until the fifth stroke, and then all she did was gasp. David tore his eyes from her stripped body to look into the mirror hanging above the mantle, and caught her defiant eyes glaring back at him. Then the sixth and final lash descended across her flesh, and although she threw her head back from the pain, she took it without complaint.

'Release her,' Monique commanded.

When the women let go of her, Leena gripped the mantel for support. The room was silent, and David glanced at George. His face was flushed with anger and pain. His beautiful wife had taken the beating he had ordered for her, and now she was about to receive a rod of a different kind.

The silence was suddenly broken by the thud of Leena's body hitting the rug; she had fainted.

Two of the women lifted her gently up into a sitting position while the third held a glass of brandy to her lips. Despite her mental defiance, Leena's young body had sought release from the torment in unconsciousness.

During this slight intermission, Monique ordered George to pour a brandy for her and for David, and instructed the women to return the furniture to its proper place. Then she and David sat down again.

'Who will go underneath her?' Monique asked.

The women glanced at one another, but no volunteers were forthcoming.

'If no one agrees, Jubal will do as he wishes.'

The women looked at the huge man, and then at each other again. Finally, a girl not much older than Leena spoke up. 'I will,' she said.

Monique looked at Jubal, and the man nodded as he began undressing.

'Where are you going?' his mistress demanded of George, who was making his way to the door. 'This is being done at your request, so that everyone can see justice has no favourites. You will stay and watch.'

Once Jubal was naked, David saw what was probably the largest erection he had ever beheld. Jubal's cock looked to be about a foot long and was equally impressive in girth. The three women stared at it with concern as they helped Leena to her feet. The other girl, the one who had volunteered, then turned away from them, and Leena's arms were wrapped around her neck from behind. The girl then knelt down in front of the fire and leaned forward until her head was touching the carpet, bringing Leena down with her. They spread her legs, and Leena was now in a position to be mounted from behind.

It was clear to David why this position was being used, because if Jubal mounted her from the front, she would have rubbed her welt-covered back and bottom on the carpet and suffered greatly.

The impressive black man got down on his knees and aimed his rigid cock towards the girl's pussy. Several times he attempted to penetrate her, but she was unresponsive. Eventually he nodded at one of the women, who crouched down and spread Leena's labia open. Jubal finally got his helmet inserted, and then he slowly sank every last inch of his enormous erection inside her.

For about ten minutes he penetrated the girl with all the passion and ferocity she had been missing in her marriage. The execution of the punishment was almost methodical, but Jubal's violent fucking was not, and it aroused David where he sat uncomfortably in his chair trying to hide the hard-on in his trousers. Occasionally he glanced at Monique, only to find her looking impassively at the scene whilst calmly smoking another cigarette and sipping her brandy.

David was almost relieved when Jubal's neck thickened, and his whole body shuddered as he fired his sperm into the young wife's belly. A moment later he pulled out of her, got to his feet and walked across to his mistress. He stood quietly in front of her as Monique leaned forward and studied his rigid penis. She blew a cloud of cigarette smoke over the black shaft, and then looked up into his equally dark eyes.

'Well done, Jubal,' she said quietly. 'The girls will take Leena back to your hut now. I will let George know when he can have her back.'

The women helped a semi-conscious Leena to her feet, and escorted her from the room while Jubal put his clothes back on.

'Now, George,' Monique said, 'you can tell the village that your mistress shows favours to no one. Everyone is equal here under the law.'

George nodded and made another attempt to leave the room, but his mistress called him back yet again.

'When Leena returns to you, she will be carrying. You must prepare your hut for the new arrival.'

'Yes, madam, I will. Thank you,' he said, and was finally allowed to leave.

Only David and Monique were left in the room, and David was full of anticipation, but his erection instantly deflated when Monique announced she was exhausted from the night's activities and was going to bed.

'You must stay the night,' she told him. 'I haven't forgotten my promise to fly you to Miami tomorrow. I will drive you back to the city in the morning, and you can pick up your things then.'

David was roused from a deep and dreamless sleep by breakfast, carried into his room by Maisey. She had brought him eggs-over-easy, bacon, toast, and strawberry preserves.

She greeted him cheerfully, and placed the tray on a desk before pulling back the drapes and opening the windows. Sunshine streamed into the room, along with a riot of noise from outside indicating work was already well underway on the plantation.

When Maisey left, he got out of bed and picked up a piece of toast. He intended to take a few bites and then head for the bathroom, but the view outside held him enthralled. Perhaps a hundred people were milling around in the vast field surrounding the house carrying bundles and otherwise going about their work. Where the Gulf met the land a jetty cut into the water. It had been invisible by night, but now David saw a boat tied to it that the villagers were loading with bails of cotton.

Eventually he headed for the bathroom and showered as quickly as possible, eager to get outside.

Monique was sitting out on the veranda looking busy and efficient and absolutely stunning in a white pantsuit. She was drinking orange juice at a long table while signing some documents the captain of the boat had brought her.

212

'Good morning, David.' She smiled up at him. 'Did you sleep well?'

'Yes, thank you, like a log… good morning.' He reached out and shook the captain's hand. 'This is wonderful!' he exclaimed. 'It's like being transported back into the past.'

'Yes, it is.' Monique rolled up the papers, and handed them back to the captain. 'That should do it,' she said. 'See you in another two weeks.'

The man smiled at her, saluted David, and headed for the water.

'I telephoned the airport early this morning,' Monique told him. 'They said the plane would be ready by three o'clock. Would you like some orange juice?'

On the way to *The Lafayette* to pick up his things, David remembered the RV. He had been planning to drive around to used car lots and sell it before catching his flight to Miami, but he really did not need the money the vehicle would fetch. It took some doing, but he finally persuaded Monique to accept it as payment for the flight. She admitted the plantation needed a new truck, and said she would trade the RV in for one when the time came.

Jubal took the RV back to the plantation, and Monique drove them to the airport. It was little more than a runway surrounded by a handful of small buildings.

She waved at the lone security guard and drove into one of the hangars, inside which sat a small white plane with twin engines. A man was busy cleaning its windows.

Monique jumped eagerly out of the Land Rover. 'All done, Joe?' she asked.

The man smiled at her before pushing the rag into a pocket of his overalls. 'Everything's dandy, Miss Petain, got straight to her the second you called.'

213

'That's good, Joe, thank you. There's some parcels in the trunk. Would you be a dear and load them up for me? I've just got to go see Joe senior so he can log in my flight plans.'

David had little in the way of belongings except his computer, a suitcase full of clothes, and a second suitcase stuffed with money. The other parcels belonged to Monique.

'There you go, mister,' Joe said after he had finished loading the plane. 'Have a good flight.'

David thanked him, and then stood around for about another twenty minutes waiting for Monique to return.

'Sorry, David,' she apologised when she finally reappeared. 'There are so many formalities to attend to before they let you take off. We'll be on our way in a few minutes. You go park the car in the lot and I'll meet you out near the runway. I've got a long list of checks to run through before we can take off.'

David had flown many times before, though only on commercial airliners. The intimacy of the small plane, and sitting next to the pilot, gave this journey an added touch of excitement, and he climbed into his seat with childlike enthusiasm.

'First time in a private plane?' Monique asked him indulgently when she saw his smiling face.

He nodded.

'Well, let me tell you, the fun never wears off.' She hit the throttle, and David jerked in his seat as the plane lurched forward onto the runway. The engine screamed, his heart thumped, and the ground fell away.

'Miami, we're on our way!' Monique exclaimed with infectious excitement.

The noise of the engines was surprisingly loud, but it

eventually faded into a background drone as the plane reached cruising altitude. The sights below them were breathtaking. Green islands studded the blue waters of the gulf, and huge flocks of birds took to the skies, disturbed by the engine's unmelodious rattle.

'This is quite an experience for me,' David said with feeling. 'I don't know how to repay you.'

'I think you already have. Running the plantation is very hard work. It's so easy to forget you have a life.' She adjusted some controls and, to David's alarm, got out of her seat and made her way to the rear of the plane. 'Don't worry,' she smiled at him over her shoulder, 'it's not only jumbo jets that possess the marvels of modern navigation. We're quite safe.' She flipped open a hamper, and pulled out a bottle of champagne along with some cheese and crackers. 'Here,' she said, 'hold this.'

David took the bottle from her, and watched as she prepared a small picnic on one of the seats.

'That's quite a feast,' he complimented her. 'I don't think we'll eat it all. What's in the other case?'

'That's for my return journey. We've got some hours before us yet.' She handed him a glass, and poured him some champagne. 'Help yourself.'

David got out of his seat and joined her in the back. He took a sandwich, and while he was eating it, he watched the throttle stick moving by itself up in the cockpit. It was an eerie feeling to be up in the air having a picnic and drinking champagne with no one flying the plane.

'When do you return to England?' Monique asked him between bites.

David kept his eyes on the stick. 'I don't know if I ever will.'

'You have no one waiting for you there? No job? No

responsibilities?'

He looked out of a window. There was nothing but miles of ocean below them. 'No. I was going to settle in Miami and enjoy the sun, but now I'm not so sure.'

'You've been bitten by the travel bug.' She winked at him, and then kicked off her shoes, leaned back in her seat, and put her feet up on the pilot's chair. 'I'm not so lucky. I have many people who rely on me. To get away like this is so wonderful. I wish I could travel all my life.'

'Oh, travelling came relatively late in life for me. I took a job in Pakistan years ago and, well, things just seemed to escalate from there. I never planned to travel like this, it just happened.'

'You're very lucky,' Monique insisted fervently. 'That's why I came to your table last night. Luck has blessed you.'

'Yes, it has.' He leaned forward and kissed her lips, which were pink today.

He had made love in many places, but this was the first time he had done so floating up in the sky. The environment was unique, and the danger only enhanced the excitement. Monique undressed slowly, revealing more and more of her lovely body between mouthfuls of cheese and sips of wine. They ate, drank and made love as the plane cut across the sky. For hours the purring cabin travelled between sea and sky while its two passengers enjoyed each other, and for the duration of that flight, they were the only two people left alive.

Then suddenly the radio crackled and a voice called out. The sound startled them both, but then Monique giggled and slipped naked into the pilot's seat to speak with the Miami control tower. As she was talking to them, David kissed her neck and fondled her breasts.

The tower gave her instructions about which runway to

use, and Monique replied that she understood. Her voice was calm, her manner professional again, and David respected the change in her behaviour. He passed her clothes to her, and then gathered up his own. Soon they were both dressed, and the remains of their picnic had been packed away. He then returned to the co-pilot's seat and they began their descent.

When they had landed safely, they taxied onto a small runway where a row of other small planes sat beneath the penetrating sunlight.

Monique smiled at him. 'Welcome to Miami, David.'

'Are you coming to meet my friend?' he asked her. 'I'm sure he would be delighted to meet you.'

She shook her head. 'I have to buy some more fuel and register for my trip back. If I stay away too long, who'll run the plantation? Besides, we can't all be as free as a bird.'

David leaned forward and kissed her lips one last time. Then he climbed out of the plane and on to the next leg of his journey.

More exciting titles available from Chimera

* * *

All **Chimera** titles are available from your local bookshop or newsagent, or direct from our mail order department. Please send your order with your credit card details, a cheque or postal order (made payable to *Chimera Publishing Ltd*) to: **Chimera Publishing Ltd., Readers' Services, PO Box 152, Waterlooville, Hants, PO8 9FS**. Or call our **24 hour telephone/fax credit card hotline: +44 (0)23 92 783037** (Visa, Mastercard, Switch, JCB and Solo only).

To order, send: Title, author, ISBN number and price for each book ordered, your full name and address, cheque or postal order for the total amount, and include the following for postage and packing:
UK and BFPO: £1.00 for the first book, and 50p for each additional book to a maximum of £3.50.
Overseas and Eire: £2.00 for the first book, £1.00 for the second and 50p for each additional book.

*Titles £5.99. All others £4.99

For a copy of our free catalogue please write to:

Chimera Publishing Ltd
Readers' Services
PO Box 152
Waterlooville
Hants
PO8 9FS

or email us at:
sales@chimerabooks.co.uk

or purchase from our range of superb titles at:
www.chimerabooks.co.uk

Sales and Distribution in the USA and Canada

LPC Group
Client Distribution Services
193 Edwards Drive
Jackson
TN 38301
USA

Sales and Distribution in Australia

Dennis Jones & Associates Pty Ltd
19a Michellan Ct
Bayswater
Victoria
Australia 3153

* * *